"You could marry me instead."

Aria scowled at him. "That's not funny."

The words Ethan hadn't meant to say hung in the air between them. His mouth was dry. "Is it really two and a half million dollars?"

"Yes. Harmon offered to give Dad the money if I would marry him."

"Bastard."

"At least Harmon wants what I want. He wants children, and he's willing to put a ring on my finger."

"So am I," Ethan said quietly. "Well, not the kid part. And probably not the real marriage. But I am willing to put an engagement ring on your finger temporarily. And I'm willing to pay back every cent that slimy opportunist gave your father in exchange for buying himself a bride."

"Why would you do that?"

Of all the answers he could have given her, none was as dangerous as the truth.

* * *

Hot Texas Nights by
USA TODAY bestselling author
Janice Maynard is part of the
Texas Cattleman's Club: Houston series.

Dear Reader,

It's always an incredible honor being asked to participate in a Texas Cattleman's Club continuity series. I'm especially proud this month to be kicking off a new TCC story that will expand the popular franchise from Royal, Texas, to Houston!

Years ago, long before I was a published author, I loved reading the Texas Cattleman's Club books written by some of my very favorite authors. Dixie Browning was one in particular. I even sent her an old-school letter asking for advice, and she was kind enough to respond.

That's just one example of how wonderful it is to be part of the supportive romance community. Readers and writers, all celebrating the power of love.

Even though the characters in the Texas Cattleman's Club stories are fictional, the themes of family and drama, betrayal and forgiveness, are timeless and true.

Come with us now on a new Texas Cattleman's Club journey...a book a month through November 2019. We promise you love and laughter, high-stakes twists and turns, and plenty of hot, sexy heroes.

Thanks for reading and loving Harlequin Desire!

Janice Maynard

JANICE MAYNARD

——

HOT TEXAS NIGHTS

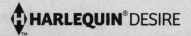

Special thanks and acknowledgment are given to
Janice Maynard for her contribution to the Texas
Cattleman's Club: Houston series.

For Hattie,
the newest member of our clan.
We love your sweet smile and your
independent spirit. ☺

ISBN-13: 978-1-335-60349-4

Recycling programs
for this product may
not exist in your area.

Hot Texas Nights

This edition published by arrangement with Harlequin Books S.A.

For questions and comments about the quality of this book,
please contact us at CustomerService@Harlequin.com.

Printed in U.S.A.

USA TODAY bestselling author **Janice Maynard** loved books and writing even as a child. After multiple rejections, she finally sold her first manuscript! Since then, she has written fifty-plus books and novellas. Janice lives in Tennessee with her husband, Charles. They love hiking, traveling and family time. You can connect with Janice at www.janicemaynard.com, www.Twitter.com/janicemaynard, www.Facebook.com/janicemaynardreaderpage and www.Instagram.com/janicemaynard.

Books by Janice Maynard

Harlequin Desire

The Kavanaghs of Silver Glen

A Not-So-Innocent Seduction
Baby for Keeps
Christmas in the Billionaire's Bed
Twins on the Way
Second Chance with the Billionaire
How to Sleep with the Boss
For Baby's Sake

Southern Secrets

Blame It On Christmas

Texas Cattleman's Club: Houston

Hot Texas Nights

Visit her Author Profile page at Harlequin.com, or janicemaynard.com, for more titles.

Don't miss a single book in the
Texas Cattleman's Club: Houston series!

Hot Texas Nights
by *USA TODAY* bestselling author
Janice Maynard

Wild Ride Rancher
by *USA TODAY* bestselling author
Maureen Child

That Night in Texas
by Joss Wood

Rancher in Her Bed
by *USA TODAY* bestselling author
Joanne Rock

Married in Name Only
by *USA TODAY* bestselling author
Jules Bennett

Off Limits Lovers
by Reese Ryan

Texas-Sized Scandal
by *USA TODAY* bestselling author
Katherine Garbera

Tangled with a Texan
by *USA TODAY* bestselling author
Yvonne Lindsay

Hot Holiday Rancher
by *USA TODAY* bestselling author
Catherine Mann

One

Ethan Barringer was on top of the world. After months of late nights, endless negotiations and an almost unbearable workload, his drive and focus had finally paid off big-time. Perry Construction had won the bid to renovate the building that would become a brand-new Cattleman's Club in Houston, Texas. Although seventy-year-old Sterling Perry owned the company—and would likely claim all the credit for the coup—Ethan, Sterling's CEO, basked in the satisfaction of knowing he himself had made it happen.

He rolled a chilled bottle of beer between his fingertips, his right knee bouncing restlessly beneath the table. Adrenaline pumped through his veins. The irony didn't escape him. If there was ever a time for celebration, this was it. But he had neglected his social life so completely during the last few months that there was no one on hand to raise a glass with him tonight.

He had come to the Royal Diner because it was a comfortable hangout, and because no one would remark on a man dining alone. After polishing off a huge, medium-rare sirloin with all the trimmings and a decadent piece of homemade lemon icebox pie, he was now faced with the prospect of a long, empty evening ahead of him.

Tomorrow he would fly to Houston and wouldn't be back for at least six weeks. Though he kept a secondary residence here in Royal, his home and office were in Houston. He tended to bounce back and forth between the big city and the small town of his birth. Each had its own charm.

He loved the anonymity of the always-busy metropolis. But nothing could replace the feeling of belonging he experienced whenever his work brought him back to Royal.

Suddenly, the diner door blew open. Someone had tried to come inside, but a gust of mid-January wind practically jerked the plate glass from its hinges. Amid a flurry of chilled air and feminine pique, the diner's latest customer finally appeared. She leaned against the entrance and smoothed her hair.

Amanda Battle, the sheriff's wife who owned the diner, lifted a hand and smiled. "Hey, Aria. Sorry about that. You look frozen to the bone. If you're not meeting anyone, come sit at the counter and talk to me."

Though the new arrival didn't glance in Ethan's direction, he recognized her immediately. Aria Jensen.

Five feet four inches tall. Eyes as blue as the wide Texas skies. Long wavy blond hair that was decidedly tousled at the moment. And enough curves to make a guy sit up and take notice.

His groin tightened. All work and no play made a man hungry. And not just for Amanda Battle's incredible desserts.

Ethan eavesdropped unashamedly.

Amanda brought Aria a cup of coffee and a list of the day's specials. "What brings you out on such a nasty evening?"

"Starvation, mainly." The younger woman shed her coat with a grin and draped it across the red faux-leather stool beside her. The 1950s-themed eatery had booths that matched the stools, and a black-and-white checkerboard linoleum floor. Though the clock over the soda fountain said it was only six thirty, the diner was on the empty side tonight. Most people were probably hunkered down at home. Winters in Royal, Texas, weren't usually too bad, but this week's weather had been blustery and cold.

Amanda nodded. "I understand. At the end of a long workday, no woman I know wants to cook. I'm glad you stopped by."

Aria sipped her coffee and pointed at the menu. "I'll take a number three. I need comfort food."

Ethan glanced at the small bundle of menus tucked behind the sugar canister on his table. Aria had ordered a grilled cheese with vegetable soup. Not much had changed over the years.

Following an impulse that drove him to his feet, he

crossed the small room and tapped her on the shoulder. "Hey, stranger. I've finished eating, but I could use some company. You want to join me?"

The stool turned. Big, long-lashed eyes looked up at him. "Ethan. How nice to see you."

The words were cordial enough, but her expression was guarded. He and Aria had known each other since they were in grade school. Her visible hesitation nicked his pride. They had grown apart in recent years.

Again, he issued the invitation, although this time he didn't touch her. Something about her cool manner told him to keep his hands to himself. "Come sit with me," he cajoled. "We can catch up."

Amanda unwittingly aided his cause. "Go ahead," she said. "I'll bring the food to you over there when it's ready. It's not like I'm being run off my feet tonight."

Aria smiled at the diner owner. "Thanks." She scooped up her coat and purse and followed Ethan to his booth. Her cheeks were pink. The color *could* be a reaction to the warmth of the diner after being outside in the cold, or Aria might be feeling uncomfortable.

That idea bothered him. There had been a time years ago when he'd thought he and Aria might end up in the midst of a hot-and-heavy relationship, but he had pulled himself back from the edge in the nick of time. The petite woman had "happily-ever-after" written all over her. The prospect of domesticity gave Ethan the hives.

Even so, he was happy to see her now. He waited until she was settled, and then he sat down. Amanda brought him a second beer and refilled Aria's white porcelain coffee mug. After that, the two of them were alone…or as alone as two people could be in a public place.

He smiled at her. "You look good, Aria."

"Thanks. You, too."

"Is there a man in your life these days? I haven't talked to you in a couple of years."

"Probably longer," she said, the words matter-of-fact. "You're in Houston most of the time, and I work two jobs."

Something buzzed between them in the silence. Something that kept him on edge. An awareness. The reference to her employment was not about needing money in the bank. She wasn't destitute. Her family's sporting-goods business did well in Royal. More importantly, Aria was the executive administrator at the Texas Cattleman's Club.

"Are you happy?" he asked. The question tumbled from his lips uncensored. He had denied himself the pleasure of a relationship with her years ago because he thought he was doing her a favor. Now he wondered if his sacrifice had been pointless.

His own father had cheated on his mother repeatedly. Ethan had been afraid he shared those genes. So he kept his relationships with the opposite sex brief and unemotional.

Yet here he was, craving a stroll down memory lane with a woman who had seen him at his best and his worst over the years.

She nodded slowly, telling him that his inner monologue had not been as long as it seemed. "I *am* happy," she said firmly. "My life is great."

"Good. Good…" Holy hell. He sounded like a geriatric uncle.

Amanda arrived with Aria's food. "Enjoy," she said, giving Ethan an odd look before she walked away.

Aria fell on the sandwich and soup as if she hadn't eaten in days. Her enthusiasm and the way she enjoyed the simple meal gave Ethan some seriously weird feelings. Was she that passionate in bed when a man was pleasuring her? His throat dried, and the front of his pants tightened.

Surely it was bizarre to be turned on by a woman eating soup.

His companion seemed oblivious to his consternation. She licked a smidge of cheese from the edge of her mouth and eyed him over the rim of her coffee cup. "What about you, Ethan? I hear great things about your job in Houston. Though I'm positive that working for Sterling Perry is no picnic."

He laughed roughly, feeling the stress of the last ten weeks begin to lift. Steering the behemoth of a ship that was Perry Holdings consumed his life. "You could say that. But he and I get along reasonably well."

"Probably because you aren't related to him," Aria said wryly.

"True." Sterling's four adult children had complicated relationships with their father.

"I heard some exciting news floating around the club today," Aria said.

"It's true. I found out just this afternoon that our construction division has been awarded the contract to renovate the new Texas Cattleman's Club site in Houston. I'm pretty pumped." An understatement, for sure.

For the first time, Aria gave him an open, uncomplicated smile. "That's fabulous," she said, beaming at him. "I'm so happy for you."

Her genuine response and the wattage of her smile warmed him despite the lousy weather. "I wasn't sure it was going to happen," he admitted.

"So why are you here in Royal?"

"Well, I've had a few meetings with the TCC board members, making sure we have a vision for what they want. Going forward now, I'll be in Houston mostly, but bouncing back and forth."

"I was surprised to hear it's a renovation. I've been out of town off and on and missed part of the debate. Why not build from scratch?"

"Ryder Currin found a stellar building on a prime downtown corner in Houston. It was a luxury boutique hotel that went under during the recession. The place fell into disrepair."

"And now you're going to give it a makeover."

"From the ground up."

Aria's enthusiasm washed over him like a benediction. He'd be lying if he said the project was going to be smooth sailing. Though Sterling Perry had won the bid to do the reconstruction, his archrival, the much younger Ryder Currin, had actually been the driving force behind setting up a branch of Royal's famous club in Houston.

Now both men wanted control. There was bad blood

between them, and there would likely be plenty of collateral damage.

Ethan tapped his fingers on the table, still itchy from that pesky adrenaline…and something more elemental—an intense physical awareness that he had always experienced around Aria. "You should come," he said suddenly. "When we begin to make progress, I'll show you around."

She blinked at him. "Come to Houston?"

He cocked his head. "It's not all that far," he drawled. "We have these newfangled things called jets."

"Very funny." Her cheeks turned pink again. "I'd enjoy that."

Something in her gaze increased his discomfort. He liked to think of Aria as a childhood friend. Yet nothing about this woman was childlike. She was sexy and adorable in her complete femininity. He could think of at least a dozen ways he wanted to strip her naked and see what happened next.

She reached across the table and took his hand, surprising the hell out of him. "I'm so proud of you, Ethan. This is huge."

The touch of her slender fingers on his larger, rougher hand sent a lightning bolt of lust to his sex. "I wanted to celebrate," he admitted huskily. "But I've cut myself off from my friends for a long time."

"Because you're a workaholic."

It wasn't a question. He curled his hand around hers. "It's all I have," he said. "I'm ambitious. Nobody gets ahead in this world if they don't give a hundred and ten percent."

"And you don't want anything else?"

Her quiet question stole his breath. *Hell, yes*. He wanted plenty. But Aria was off-limits. She was sweet and wholesome, and she wanted babies and a ring on her finger.

"Life is all about choices," he said, stroking her palm. He couldn't quite meet her gaze. He was concerned she would see his physical hunger and be put off by his response to her…and to their physical connection.

"Or maybe you're just afraid." She pulled her hand away, leaving him bereft. The tart, pointed attack startled him.

"I'm not afraid of anything," he protested.

Aria crossed her arms, drawing attention to her softly rounded breasts. She was wearing a pale pink cashmere turtleneck. The color should have washed her out, but instead, she glowed like a winter rose.

Their hushed standoff lasted mere seconds, though it felt like forever. Amanda came to clear the table, seemingly oblivious to the undercurrents that swirled about them.

When they were alone again, Aria gave him a wicked, mocking smile. "Prove it," she said.

He felt befuddled, perhaps by the fact that all the blood in his body had rushed south. "Prove what?"

"That you're not afraid."

There was no avoiding her challenge. Had he ever known her at all, or had she changed? This was a sexual gauntlet, thrown down by the woman he had thought was passive…perhaps even repressed.

Her sharp-eyed gaze said otherwise. Beneath the

fuzzy fabric of her sweater, her nipples budded tightly, signaling her response to their verbal foreplay. His forehead beaded with sweat. "Well, I—"

"I have champagne at my house," she said quietly. "It was supposed to be for my parents' anniversary, but they took off on a cruise, and we never had a party for them. The bottle has been collecting dust. I'd like to pop the cork in your honor tonight. What do you say?"

What he was *supposed* to say was *no*. Nothing had changed. He and Aria were longtime friends. Sex was not on the table.

Could he go to her house, drink a single glass of champagne to celebrate his big day and then go home?

Doubtful. But he was going to do it, anyway. Because he couldn't resist her smile. Or the naughty twinkle in her eyes. Or the way she smelled—like vanilla and something darker, more sensual.

"Sure," he croaked. "I guess I've got time for one glass. Are you still at the same address?"

"Still there," she said. She slipped her arms into her coat and signed the credit-card slip Amanda had unobtrusively placed on the table.

Ethan frowned. "I should have bought your dinner," he said. "I wasn't paying attention." The truth was, he'd been so focused on Aria that he never even noticed her taking her credit card out of her purse.

"Don't be silly. This isn't a date." She slid out of the booth and stood, fluffing her hair out over the collar of her winter jacket. In addition to the sweater, she was wearing jeans and black leather, knee-high boots with three-inch heels that boosted her modest height. "I'll meet you at my place." And then she was gone, whisked out the door on another blast of cold air.

Ethan stood as well, feeling as if he'd been hit over the head with a board. What just happened?

He made his way to the counter. "Hey, Amanda. You never brought me my check."

The attractive diner owner grinned. "Aria bought your dinner."

He gaped. "How? Why?"

"She scribbled a note on her check. Said she wanted to celebrate your big coup. I heard about the new project. Congratulations."

"Word travels fast," he muttered.

"Well, it does in Royal, that's for sure."

Ethan left the diner in a daze. Something pulled at him, some inexorable force. Call it destiny or curiosity or plain male lust. Whatever it was, he couldn't ignore its appeal.

He was headed for Aria Jensen's house, and the two of them were going to drink champagne.

The drive was short. Less than fifteen minutes. When he pulled up in front of the bungalow-style home, there was a parking space at the curb. This section of Royal dated back to the 1930s. Many of the houses had been renovated and restored to their original glory.

Aria's was brick with white trim and a wraparound porch. He spotted two rocking chairs and half a dozen empty planters that would be splashed with color in a few months.

It was the kind of house that would be perfect for a family with a dog or a cat and two-point-five precocious toddlers. It wasn't even a stretch for Ethan to imagine Aria cooking something delightful in a cozy kitchen or reading bedtime stories to a son or a daughter with sun-bleached curls.

His stomach clenched.

He should turn around and get back in his car. Right now.

Every reason he had stayed away from Aria in the past still existed. He wanted her. He always had. But he'd be bad for her.

When they were children at school, he had kept the bullies at bay and let her be the irrepressible tomboy she wanted to be. He'd protected her and cared for her and made sure she was always safe and happy.

But when they became teenagers and then adults, he discovered the painful truth about his father's many liaisons. His mother hadn't spilled her guts. But Ethan had found her crying one day and had done his own detective work. The truth had curdled his stomach.

After that, whenever he had been tempted to have his way with the luscious Aria, he had stayed away. For her own good...

Two

Aria kicked off her boots and put on a pair of warm bunny slippers. She told herself she wasn't going to primp for Ethan Barringer. Even so, she tidied her windblown hair, spritzed the tiniest bit of perfume between her breasts and brushed her teeth.

She didn't have long.

Just as she scuttled back downstairs, her doorbell rang. Placing a hand on her jumpy stomach, she took a deep breath. Nothing was going to happen. Ethan was a longtime friend. A sexy, gorgeous, unavailable friend.

When she let him in, he smelled like the outdoors. Crisp and fresh and manly. She took his coat, hung it on a wooden peg nearby and waved him toward her comfy living room. "Make yourself at home," she said. "I'll grab the champagne and the glasses."

She was gone less than five minutes. When she returned, Ethan had his eyes closed, his head leaned back against the sofa and his sock-clad feet propped on her wormy chestnut coffee table. She'd bought the solid piece of furniture at an antiques fair in Austin. It was casual and chic, and to be honest, it cried out for a man's big feet.

The silly thought made her smile inwardly.

"Here we go," she said.

Ethan looked amazing, though exhausted. He didn't even hear her three softly spoken words, poor man. His shoulders strained the seams of a navy-and-green tattersall shirt. Dark khakis molded to powerful, masculine thighs. His navy linen sport coat was unbuttoned.

As she watched, his flat abdomen rose and fell with the rhythm of his breathing. His short dark hair had been cut recently. A day's growth of beard shadowed his masculine jaw.

Perhaps she should be insulted that a man—on the cusp of spending an evening with her—had fallen asleep so rapidly. In truth, though, his comfort in her home was touching.

Ethan had always been a huge part of her life. At least until five years ago, when his work had taken him away from Royal. Even when he'd come home for the holidays, something had changed. He'd grown distant, careful, around her.

At first, she'd thought it was because he had found someone to be serious about, and perhaps that other woman didn't want him spending time with Aria. The truth was more daunting and less easily understood.

Ethan didn't *have* relationships. At least not in Royal. Presumably there were women in Houston. But the gossip mill characterized even those rumored liaisons as one-night stands. Strictly physical. Nothing more.

He was alone, and he liked it that way.

Aria sat down beside him deliberately, leaving only three or four feet between them. Ethan Barringer was the reason she had found every other romantic relationship in her life to be dull and uninspired. Her longtime crush on him was keeping her from having the kind of life she wanted and deserved. Maybe tonight's meeting was serendipity. Or karma.

The time for being a passive, well-behaved female was over. *Something* existed between Ethan and her. She was prepared to find out what it was, even if the prospect made her shiver with nerves.

What she contemplated was the equivalent of poking a stick into a lion's cage. You thought you were safe, but the beast might break loose and devour you.

"Ethan." She said his name a bit louder.

He jerked and scrubbed his hands over his face. "Sorry about that," he muttered. "I've been running on caffeine and four hours' sleep."

"No worries." She handed him the bottle of champagne. "You should open it. I don't have much experience in that area."

He shot her a glance. "And you think I do?" But he took the bottle, anyway.

Their fingers brushed. Her throat dried.

Ethan wrestled with the wire and the foil. "Shouldn't we do this in the kitchen in case it makes a mess?"

She put a hand on his thigh—quite deliberately—and felt the warmth of his taut muscle. "I'm prepared to live dangerously tonight."

Ethan stood up abruptly to wrestle with the champagne, causing her hand to fall away. Had he done it on purpose? His cheekbones were flushed with a slash of red. She could swear when she'd said the word *dangerously* he flinched.

There was a loud pop, and the cork shot across the room. Ethan grabbed a glass. "I was afraid this would happen." He rapidly poured the foaming liquid into two flutes.

Aria used the dish towel she had brought along and mopped up the small puddle. "It's fine."

Ethan handed her a glass. "Ladies first."

She lifted her flute and clinked it against his. "To you, Ethan. Kudos for all your hard work and everything you've achieved. Perry Construction is lucky to have you."

His smile was sheepish but pleased. "Thanks, Aria."

Their gazes locked as they each drained a glass. Though Aria was no connoisseur, this particular vintage was perfect for her taste. She had spent a lot on this bottle since it was supposed to be for a party. Now she was glad. "You're welcome," she said softly. "I'm happy we ran into each other. No one should have to celebrate alone."

His Adam's apple bobbed. Noticeably. "More?" he asked, the word low and hoarse.

She nodded, holding out her glass. "It's good, isn't it? I've always heard that the bubbles can make you sneeze, but I've never had that reaction at all. I like champagne."

"Most people do," he said drily. "Or at least they pretend they do. Why else would it have a reputation for kicking off celebrations?"

He cupped his hand around hers to steady the glass as he filled it a second time. "This will be it for me," she said firmly, trying to pretend that she wasn't totally flustered by the way he touched her.

He raised an eyebrow as he released her and refilled his own glass. "No head for alcohol?"

"I'm pretty much a lightweight," she admitted as she took a sip. "I don't metabolize it rapidly enough. Makes me a cheap date, though."

Again, he raised his glass, his gaze hooded as he stared at her. "There's never been anything *cheap* about you, Aria. You're a class act all the way."

The unexpected compliment startled her. Was that arousal she saw in his eyes? Hunger she heard in his voice?

She'd only had a glass and a half of champagne. She was in complete control of her choices and her behavior. But her emotions were something else entirely. Suddenly, an almost overwhelming yearning crashed over her like a tsunami, carrying everything away in its path.

For a moment, she was sixteen again. That was the age she had been when she'd first fallen in love with Ethan Barringer. Her parents had told her it was puppy love and that she would grow out of it. Her friends had told her he was older and too sophisticated to ever think seriously about a girl like her.

But Aria *knew* Ethan. She knew his caring and his protective chivalry, for lack of a better word. She knew his honor and his devotion to his mother. And she knew the way he looked at her when he thought she wouldn't see.

All the way through the remainder of high school and the four years she'd spent away at college she'd carried her love for him. When she'd returned to Royal, Ethan had been back, as well. A man...no longer a boy.

It had seemed like the time might finally be right for her and Ethan to get together. But she'd been too bashful to make a move, and Ethan had never given any indication he was interested in her romantically. He'd been friendly. But distant. He'd kept any softer emotions he might possess locked away.

His new, blunt-edged masculinity put a wall between them. He wasn't approachable anymore. For several years, she'd mooned after him, and then he was gone to Houston.

It had been a difficult time in her life. She'd had to take a long, hard look at herself. Eventually, she'd made peace with the truth. Ethan wasn't for her. Maybe he never had been.

In the intervening years she'd dated several men. Nice guys with steady jobs and no apparent aversion to settling down eventually. But something had always been missing. Only two boyfriends had made it into her bed. The sex had been nice. Pleasurable. Not earth-shaking. She'd finally decided that she had let herself be brainwashed by books and movies.

There was no such thing as a soul mate.

Now, a chance encounter with a man she had known

since she was nine years old threatened to shred her hard-won peace.

Ethan poured himself one last glass. The bottle was almost empty. He held it up with a question on his face. She shook her head and said, "The rest is yours." He outweighed her significantly. It wouldn't hurt him to drink the last of the champagne on his own.

She set her empty crystal flute on the coffee table and watched as he finished the sparkling golden liquid. Moments later, he abandoned his glass, as well.

Ethan was here. In her house. In touching distance. The attraction they had danced around for more than a decade could be explored without interruption. Could she do it? Could she seduce this man? Before she lost her nerve, she launched herself at him. Her arms went around his waist. Her lips found his, and she kissed him recklessly.

He tasted like a dream come true. She had imagined this moment a million times. Now here she was. Nestled against his hard, warm chest.

Scant moments later, reality intruded with a sickening thud, dragging her back to earth.

Ethan had gone rigid. His lips didn't move beneath hers. His arms were stiff at his sides.

She staggered backward, her face hot with mortification. She wiped her mouth with the back of her hand as if she could erase her incredible faux pas. "Oh, damn, I'm sorry. I misread the signals. My bad."

She was babbling, but she had never been so embarrassed in her life. And so hurt.

Ethan had actually gone white beneath his year-round bronzed skin. "Aria?"

She held out a hand, palm up, staving off any unexpected movement on his part. "Just go. Please. I don't know what I was thinking."

The urge to flee was almost overpowering, but they were in *her* house. What if he tried to follow her? She couldn't bear it. This was far more dreadful than any reaction she could have envisioned on his part.

Ethan wasn't attracted to her. She had let a stupid infatuation blind her to that fact.

Tears welled in her eyes, tears she was determined not to shed. A woman could only endure so much humiliation.

He took a step forward. Only one. But she froze. "Go," she begged. "Don't make this any worse."

His jaw was like iron. His eyes blazed with some strong emotion she couldn't decipher. "Damn, Aria. Give me a minute to catch up. I've spent most of my adult life trying to stay away from you. You surprised me. That's all. Lord, yes, I want you. I've wanted you for years. But I've always known that touching you would be a mistake."

Her stomach knotted. "Why?"

He came to her and cupped her face in his hands. "Because once I start, I won't want to stop. Is that clear enough for you?"

"Oh."

He kissed her hard, his groan reverberating through both of them. "Are you sure about this?"

She was trembling so hard, she felt sick. "I want you to have sex with me, Ethan."

There. She'd said it out loud. A confident woman who went after what she wanted.

He cursed beneath his breath, then took her mouth with drugging sensuality. His lips made love to hers. The man was one hell of a kisser. His thumbs caressed her jaw on both sides. Though he kept a relatively chaste distance between them, her body arched toward his, desperately trying to tip the scales in her favor.

When he finally gave in and pulled her close, his unmistakable erection pressed against her belly. He nipped her earlobe with sharp teeth, his breath hot on her neck. "You were a delectable teenager, but you turned into one hell of a woman."

"You never said anything."

"Because you weren't for me."

"And now?"

"You still aren't, honey. But if this is really what you want tonight, I'm your man."

Something about his words bothered her, but she was too distracted to read between the lines. Ethan was looking at her the way she had always dreamed that he would one day.

"Yes," she whispered.

His chest rose and fell sharply. "Are you protected?"

"Um, no. I haven't been seeing anyone recently."

He nodded curtly. "I have two condoms in my wallet."

Some of the shimmer and shine of the moment wavered. She wasn't sure what to do next. "Okay."

His features softened. "You can still change your mind, Aria. I didn't come over here expecting anything more than a glass of champagne, I swear. I took your invitation at face value."

"That's how I meant it," she muttered. "My recent insanity was an impulse…because I want you." She paused and swallowed hard. "But not if this is a pity thing. I'm not a charity case."

He frowned. "Why on earth would I pity you?"

She shrugged. "I don't know. It strikes me as odd that you never made a move on me before tonight."

He twined a lock of her hair around his finger, his smile enigmatic. "You never asked."

Well, heck. If she'd known it was that easy, she would have asked a long time ago. "I'm not drunk," she said firmly. "I'm not even buzzed. I know what I'm doing."

His wicked grin gave her the shakes. "I'm glad we cleared that up." He curled an arm around her waist and drew her closer. "I want you to remember every little thing I'm going to do to you," he whispered, his breath warm against the shell of her ear. "Start to finish. Including the way you're going to scream my name when I make you come."

She gaped up at him, barely breathing. No other man of her acquaintance would have the confidence to be so boldly alpha, taking charge of the situation and the moment without apology. Perhaps she should have protested his arrogance, but her legs barely supported her, and breathing took all her focus. Her thighs clenched. Damp heat at her core ached.

"You're awfully sure of yourself," she muttered.

His low laugh made gooseflesh rise on her arms where they clung to his neck. "You asked me to have sex with you, sweet thing. Trust me, I won't let you be disappointed. Even if it takes all night." He paused, for the first time seeming mildly disconcerted. "Are we taking this upstairs, or do you want to make use of this very nice sofa?"

She swallowed, trying in an insufficient instant to decide how best to proceed. That was the problem with spontaneity. No time for logical decisions. No opportunity to plan. "Here is fine," she croaked. If things went south, she could always buy a new sofa to erase the memories of this night. Letting Ethan into her bed upstairs would signal an intimacy she wasn't prepared to accept. Tonight was about closure, right?

Ethan exhaled sharply, as if he was holding himself in check. "Then here it is," he said gruffly.

He released her and stepped away, slipping his wallet from his back pocket. When he calmly tossed the small strip of condom packets on the coffee table, Aria fixated on it as if it was a tiny bomb just waiting to explode and send her neatly ordered life into a million pieces.

"We could build a fire," she said. "If you're cold. The wood is already laid out. And I have matches on the mantel." *Too much babbling, Aria.* She sucked in a breath and tried to smile. "Unless we're going to generate enough heat on our own. What do you think?"

Three

Ethan winced inwardly. Aria was nervous. Should he put a stop to this before they did something they would both regret? The answer was probably *yes*, but he couldn't make himself walk away.

He burned for her.

"No fire," he said. "Not now, anyway. I don't want to wait."

His body ached for hers in a way he hadn't experienced in a very long time. The uneasy melding of lust and tenderness sounded an alarm in his gut, but he closed his mind to the danger.

Aria was finally his. At least for this one night.

He held out a hand. "Come here, beautiful. Let me touch you."

Her pupils were dilated, the irises more navy than

cornflower in the low light. Only a single small lamp burned, and it was on the far side of the room, near the front door. The drapes were drawn. Their privacy was complete in the hushed silence of the wintry night.

Aria didn't obey his request. Instead, she lifted her arms and peeled her soft, fuzzy turtleneck over her head. Tousled blond hair fell around her shoulders. Her barely there bra was the same color as the sweater. The lacy lingerie did little to conceal her dark raspberry nipples.

Her body was pale and lovely, the skin smooth and white, her slender arms toned and fit. The waistband of her jeans rode low on her hips, exposing a tiny navel that was as sexy to him as her hesitant smile.

He sucked in a breath and shuddered as his sex went from primed and ready to hard as stone. The rush of arousal eroded his patience. Even so, he kept his distance, curious to see how far she would go.

Shifting from one foot to the other, he smiled. "Don't stop now. I'm enjoying the show."

She wrinkled her nose. "I think I'm ready for you to lend a hand, Ethan. Striptease isn't really in my repertoire."

"Too bad," he said, the words ragged. He wanted to pounce on her. Devour her. But he couldn't. He wouldn't. Instead, he went to her and folded her in his arms. Perhaps she thought it odd that he simply held her for long, aching moments. If she did, she didn't say anything.

He hadn't anticipated the immediate problem of making love to Aria. For years he had locked down his reactions to her. He'd never once let himself get close to hitting on her, no matter how much he'd wanted to.

Reversing that protocol now was throwing him off his game.

He was more accustomed to easy, recreational sex with women who had plenty of experience. Aria had been in relationships. He knew that. He had witnessed several of them, and to his shame he'd been fiercely exultant when each one had ended. Despite that, he'd felt protective of her innocent soul, her innate goodness. Even as kids, he had wanted to keep her from getting hurt. Something about Aria Jensen made him want to be her defender.

But not tonight.

A shudder worked its way through his chest. He ran his hands up and down her bare back, tracing the line of her spine. "You're sure?" he asked hoarsely, his control down to a thread.

She nipped his collarbone with sharp teeth. "I want you, Ethan. I won't change my mind, I swear."

That final assurance snapped the last of his patience. He slid his hands inside her jeans and palmed her butt. Damn, that firm, curved bottom was fine.

Aria moaned and pressed against him, the faint scent of her perfume familiar and yet intriguing. He felt like a teenager with his first woman. Out of control. Apprehensive. The delicate female in his arms was important to him. He'd cut off his arm before he would hurt her.

"I fantasized about this," he admitted, nudging her head to one side and nibbling her neck.

He felt her shock.

"You did?" she said, her tone disbelieving.

"Of course. You and I have always had this awareness between us. You know it. I know it, too. When I was in college and you were a million miles away on the other side of the country, I used to ask myself why I had let you get away. I hated all those guys who were spending time with you when I couldn't. It made me nuts."

She pulled away from him and wrapped her arms around her waist, her chin going up the slightest bit as if in defiance. "You don't have to say things like that," she said. "This is sex. I don't need pretty words. I'm an adult woman. I know all the reasons men and women climb into bed together. Maybe I haven't slept around as much as some of my friends, but I'm not naive. I'd rather you not make this something it isn't."

The blunt words didn't quite disguise her vulnerability. Though he wanted to be angry, he couldn't. She was trying so hard to protect herself. "I will never lie to you," he said quietly. "Not now. Not ever." He reached for her hand and held it against his erection. "You have this effect on me. You always have."

Her fingers flexed and curved along the outline of his rigid sex, her gaze downcast, as if she was mesmerized. "I didn't know. You always treated me like a kid sister."

Even through his pants, her touch burned him. He wanted her hands on his naked flesh. The time for rational conversation was rapidly disappearing. "Not anymore, Aria. Not tonight."

At last, her body relaxed against his. Trustingly. Completely. She linked her arms around his neck. "I'm glad," she said simply.

He scooped her up and carried her the few steps to the sofa. It was long and comfy and perfect for what he had in mind. He laid her down and sat at her hip, wondering where to start. The way she looked up at him with a tiny smile on her face told him she liked the fact that he was wildly aroused.

"Don't move," he said huskily. "And don't rush me. I'm going to unwrap you like a present." He took her arms and positioned them over her head. "After all this time, I want to savor the moment."

Aria's chest rose and fell with each shallow, rapid breath. "There's something to be said for hard and fast."

The image her words conjured up blurred his vision. His hands shook as he unfastened the button at the waist of her jeans and lowered her zipper. When he dragged the denim down to her ankles, he sucked in a breath. Her panties matched her bra, but they were smaller still. And just as transparent.

Her sex was clean-shaven, all pink and perfect. "Holy hell," he whispered, gobsmacked by lust and awe and disbelief at the fact that he was about to make Aria Jensen his lover.

"Ethan…" She moved restlessly, her ankles trapped.

He looked down and saw that she still wore fuzzy pink bunny slippers. The juxtaposition of her sexy, nearly bare body and the whimsical footwear made him chuckle. "You're adorable."

"Undress me," she begged. "Hurry."

He dispensed with everything but the two items of sheer lace. "I told you not to rush me."

Aria raised up on her elbows. "I never agreed to

that." She curled a hand behind his neck and dragged him down for a desperate kiss. "I want you."

Ethan's control snapped. For the first time, it sank in that Aria was a woman who knew her own mind. He wasn't breaking any taboos.

The realization freed him. He leaned over her, supporting his weight on one hand as he kissed her mindlessly. It was wild and sweet and incredibly arousing. He was so hard, he ached, but even so, he forced himself to take things slowly. Not for Aria, but for him.

He'd never thought this would happen. Giving in to the rush of pleasure and exhilaration was elemental… almost animalistic. He buried his face between her breasts and tried to breathe. Air rushed in and out of his lungs in harsh bursts that left him dizzy and weak.

Aria played with his hair, her fingers massaging his scalp. "I think this is the part where we both get undressed," she whispered.

He licked the slope of her breast. "My clothes are the only thing keeping me from taking you like a madman."

Perhaps she heard the raw ring of truth in his words. She tugged on his chin, forcing him to look up into her blue eyes. "I love that you want me that much, Ethan. Really I do. Don't hold back. I want it all."

He nodded jerkily, sitting up long enough to unbutton his shirt. Though he couldn't bear to break the physical connection between them, he stood and shed his clothes completely.

Aria's eyes widened. Her face and neck flushed. "Wow…"

His sex bobbed at his belly. "This first time won't

last long. You've got me pretty wired. I'll make it up to you after that."

She licked her lips. "Okay."

He grabbed her wrist and drew her to her feet. "You look damned amazing in those undies, but they have to go." With one flick of his wrist, he unfastened the bra, slid it down her arms, and tossed it aside. The last remaining piece of lingerie was no challenge at all.

Dragging her slim, soft, naked body against his taller, harder frame immediately short-circuited at least half a million synapses in his brain. "God, you feel amazing."

Her cheek rested over his heart. "So do you." She scraped his butt cheeks with her fingernails, raising gooseflesh all over his body. "You're an incredibly beautiful man, Ethan Barringer. I've always thought so."

The unexpected adjective made him wince. "Men aren't beautiful," he protested.

She leaned back in his embrace and ran her hands from his throat, down over his pecs to his waist. "*You* are," she said.

Then she touched him intimately.

His whole body began to shake. A red haze obscured his vision. Desperately, he tried not to come. "You're killing me," he gasped, his forehead beading with sweat.

"Buck up, cowboy," she drawled. "I'm just getting started."

When she sank to her knees on the plush carpet and took him in her mouth, he cursed. "No. Wait."

Aria was not to be dissuaded. She suckled the head

of his erection gently, her soft blond tresses brushing his thighs. The erotic position fed into his darkest fantasies.

He fisted his hands in her hair.

Her technique was untutored, perhaps even awkward. His body didn't seem to mind. When she took more of his shaft, he gasped. "Stop," he pleaded. "Stop."

It was too late. He came hard, the force of his climax roaring through his entire body, it seemed.

Aria was unfazed. When his knees turned to jelly, she left him to collapse on the sofa and returned with a damp cloth. Gently, she cleansed him.

He was embarrassed and spent and ridiculously stunned. How did a man get to be almost thirty years old and suddenly have the best sex of his life? Hell, he hadn't even taken her yet.

Trying to swallow the lump in his throat, he managed a smile. "You've grown up."

Aria was sitting on the carpet with her legs curled beneath her. She rested her cheek against his arm. "Had to get there sooner or later."

He played with her hair, sifting the silk between his fingers. "I didn't mean for this to happen."

She lifted her head and grinned at him. "I know."

Her smug smile amused him. "I always thought you were shy."

Aria raised one eyebrow. "Maybe you thought a lot of things that weren't true."

The prospect was both intriguing and alarming. "Can we call what just happened the overture?"

"A musical reference? I'm impressed. Maybe Houston has been good for you. All that ballet and opera and symphony."

"I'm still just a good ol' boy from Royal."

"And the CEO of a huge, influential company. That's why we're celebrating, isn't it?"

"If I'd known this was in store, I'd have worked twice as hard." He ran his thumb over her bottom lip. "You're delectable. Do you know that?"

The pink in her cheeks deepened. "Maybe you've been celibate too long. Too much work and no play?"

He leaned forward and kissed her roughly, his hand curling behind her neck to keep her still. "I'm hard again," he said. "That's not abstinence. That's all you, Aria."

She seemed surprised. His sex was as ready as it had been thirty minutes ago. He felt as if he could go forever.

Aria shrugged. "I won't quibble over *why*," she said softly. "I'm just glad you're here with me tonight."

He reached down and pulled her up on top of him, chuckling when she protested. "You can't pretend to be shy now," he drawled.

"Quit staring," she whispered, her expression half embarrassed, half intrigued.

The new position gave him an exquisite view of her body. She was straddling his hips, her knees bent behind her. The few seconds it took him to grab protection and sheathe himself seemed to last forever. He gripped her waist and lifted her. "Take me, Aria. Take me now."

Her gaze clung to his. Hesitant. Aroused. "Okay." Bracing one hand on his chest, she aligned their bodies and slowly sank down on his erection, gloving his sex in tight, wet heat.

Holy damn. Incredulously, he felt himself race toward the finish line again. No way. No way in hell. Not yet.

Carefully, he moved in her, flexing his hips, watching her face to see what she liked. Aria's eyes fluttered shut. A look of intense concentration creased her brow.

He gritted his teeth, panting. Quickly, before she could protest, he took her arms behind her back and manacled her wrists with one of his hand. "Ride me, darlin'. Get what you want. You're in control."

She sucked in a breath, her nipples tightening until they were tiny, hard nubs. "Ethan…"

The way she cried out his name raised the hair all over his body. He touched her where their bodies were joined, stroking her lightly, caressing the nerves that controlled her release. "More," he croaked. "Give us both what we want."

His intimate touch lit a flame that consumed them. Aria braced her hands on his shoulders and rode him hard. The fall of her hair blinded him. Just when he thought he was going to come a second time, Aria stilled.

As she leaned forward, the slight shift in position hit about a dozen different hot spots in his groin.

"I like this, Ethan. Why did you make us wait so long?"

He grabbed a hank of her hair and reeled her in for a desperate kiss. He wanted her to stop talking. This was no time to analyze why he had finally broken his hands-off policy with Aria. He didn't want to think about the consequences. They scared him to the core.

Her lips were soft. He angled her head and took the kiss deeper. When she squeezed his sex with her inner muscles, he groaned.

It was too much and not enough. If he had been in a bed, he would have rolled and put her under him. The sofa was too confining.

He gripped her butt and thrust upward with one hard motion. Aria's gasp energized him. Looking into her eyes was a mistake. What he saw there was everything neither of them had admitted.

Nothing was hidden—her passion, her yearning, the same deep emotion he felt.

Shoving the disturbing realization aside, he concentrated on what he knew best. The here and now. Giving Aria everything she deserved.

He slowed his strokes, clamped one arm around her waist. It was clear she was close. He wanted to make it last, but his body betrayed him.

As a dark red haze obscured his vision, he went wild, hammering into her again and again until he heard her cry out. Then he allowed himself the sweet, painful pleasure of release.

It might have been minutes or hours until his breathing slowed to anything resembling normal. Aria was a sweet weight, her body draped over his. He shifted her to one side with his back against the sofa and tucked her in the curve of his arm. In a moment he would get up. When his legs would cooperate.

Her hair tickled his chin. She reached for his hand

and linked her fingers with his. "Will you stay the night?"

His gut clenched. Everything had been perfect. He'd been mellow, happy. Completely satisfied. Until she uttered the five words that ruined it all.

Aria had always thought of heartbreak as something that happened slowly, over the course of time. When all avenues of hope had been exhausted.

Ethan's unmistakable tensing shattered her euphoria in one shocking instant.

"I can't," he said brusquely. "I have an early flight."

Her throat was scraped raw by the effort to keep emotion at bay. "Oh, right," she said. "I forgot."

She rolled to her feet and reached blindly for her clothes. If he had cared about her at all, he would have stayed all night and raced for the airport at the last possible second. That's what a romantic hero would do.

For the second time, humiliation curdled her stomach and stole her breath. She was such a fool. Weaving a fairy tale about a handsome prince. Ethan was no hero.

He stood as well, made a quick trip to the bathroom and returned minutes later. She couldn't look at him. Ruthlessly, she shoved her icy feet into the bunny slippers and sifted her fingers through her rumpled hair.

When he touched her arm, he was completely dressed, from head to toe. No more washboard abs. No gloriously naked lover.

His gaze was guarded, his expression inscrutable. "I'm sorry I have to leave."

Her chin lifted. "I don't think you are. Not really.

The Ethan I remember never liked complications. Too bad I forgot that."

Something flared in his eyes. "We can do this again. Whenever I'm in town."

She hadn't thought she could feel any worse. "Hook up, you mean? Friends with benefits. How very flattering."

Temper flashed across his boldly masculine face like the portent of a thunderstorm. "I didn't mean it like that."

Her hurt and disappointment coalesced into bitter sarcasm. "Didn't you?" She sucked in a ragged breath. "I can't be something you pick up and put down between business trips. I won't."

"Tonight was more than that."

Even in the midst of her own trauma, she could see that he was disturbed. Maybe even confused. *Too. Damn. Bad.* She stared at him with her heart and her pride in pieces at her feet. "We drank champagne. We scratched an itch. End of story. Goodbye, Ethan."

He took a step in her direction. "Aria, I…"

She held up a hand, holding him off. "Do you honestly have any interest at all in a serious, long-term relationship?"

His jaw hardened. "No."

Well, there it was. She bit down hard on her bottom lip. "It's late," she said. "I have work in the morning. Goodbye, Ethan."

For the briefest of moments, a tiny spark of hope

flickered. On his face she saw…something. Was he regretting his words?

Before she could say anything else, he turned on his heel and walked out the front door.

Four

Six weeks later

Ethan stepped back, held his hand over his eyes to block the sun and gazed at the roof. The inspector on top gave him a thumbs-up. Thank God. After a frustrating month and a half of permit snafus, asbestos removal and various other code concerns, they were finally getting close to the official ground-breaking. Soon, major renovations would turn this aging beauty with good bones into a stunning home for the Houston branch of the prestigious Texas Cattleman's Club.

Though not as old as the iconic building in Royal, this new iteration would be stately and impressive, as well. The three-story building was projected to have suites on the top floor for the president and chairman of the board. The second floor would be officers' and board members' offices, along with conference rooms. The main level would include a large ballroom, a bar/café for club members only and a central meeting hall.

Because of the relatively modest size of the new TCC, nearby hotels would serve as lodging for the members when they were in town. Undoubtedly, some of those hotels would also offer special amenities like health clubs.

Ethan felt pride as he gazed at the building. He had worked his ass off for these last six weeks he had been in Houston.

But not a single night passed that he didn't lie in bed and think about Aria. He had screwed up badly. He owed her an apology. Given his history with her, he was ashamed of how things had ended. But she wasn't making it easy for him to do penance.

She wouldn't return his calls or his texts or his emails. And Ethan didn't have the luxury of running off to Royal to take care of personal concerns. The entire success or failure of the new Cattleman's Club project rested squarely on his shoulders.

The building had to be perfect. The bar was high.

He rotated his neck, wishing he had a beer and twenty-four hours to sleep. His nights had been restless. He'd alternated between being horny and despondent.

He'd been right to stay from Aria all the years before now. Sex had ruined everything.

In the end, he resorted to writing her a letter...the old-fashioned way. He told her how special she was to him, but that he was a bad risk. They could be friends, but nothing more. He told her he would pretend their champagne-fueled night of celebration had never happened.

That last part was a blatant lie. He would *never* forget the incredible night of sex with Aria. Not if he lived until he was a hundred. The images of their intimacy were burned into his DNA.

Her stony silence during the intervening weeks told him how badly he had hurt her. It was time for him to go back to Royal very soon. He was determined to track her down and make her listen to his apology.

Then perhaps, he could move on.

Aria sat at her desk in the Texas Cattleman's Club and tried to concentrate on the pile of purchase orders in front of her, when all she wanted to do was think about Ethan. Most days, she loved her job. Becoming the executive administrator was a dream come true. Aside from her own personal ambition, the position had smoothed the way for her father to finally gain entrée into the organization he had aspired to for so long.

Her parents were longtime residents of Royal, and they both came from moneyed, well-respected families. But her father had made some enemies in his hot-headed youth. Some of those men had been successful in denying him membership.

It was only when Aria went to work for the club that she was finally able to smooth over the past discontent and bring her father on board.

Though she still occasionally had a hand in the family business, more and more her work at the TCC was keeping her busy and fulfilled.

Or at least it used to…

She tried to pull a stubborn staple out of a thick stack of papers and stabbed her finger in the process. It bled as if she'd been mortally wounded. Great. Just great. Did workman's comp cover blood loss? She knew she was in a bad mood, and she knew why. The knowledge didn't make the ache in her heart any less painful.

While she was reaching for a tissue, her phone dinged. The text was a familiar number. Ethan.

We need to talk…

She snorted, no one around to hear the derisive exclamation. No way in hell. She had ignored every one of Ethan's attempts to communicate with her, including the surprisingly old-fashioned letter. Each text and email was more painful than the last.

Ethan wanted absolution, but she wanted so much more.

Impatiently, she responded.

NO. We don't.

Surely that was clear enough for him.

She tossed the phone on her desk and sucked the end of her finger. The small puncture hurt like heck. Maybe her finger had as many nerve endings as her broken heart.

Suddenly, a male voice from the doorway interrupted her pity party. "I really think we do."

Ethan. Standing in her office. Damn.

She rolled her chair backward a few inches and summoned a noncommittal expression. "I'm busy."

"You've been ignoring me."

The man looked even better than she remembered, but he seemed tired. Maybe he had even lost a little weight.

"Not at all," she lied. "I'm sure it only seemed that way, because you've been so busy in Houston. I hear the project is going well."

He shrugged. "The usual bumps in the road. We should be able to have the ground-breaking party soon."

"Good." *Please go, please go, please go...* She couldn't bear this. "Why are you here?" she asked bluntly.

"You know why." His jaw turned to granite. "We didn't settle things between us when I left town."

"Oh, yes, we did. We settled the heck out of it."

He scrubbed his hands over his face. His jaw was shadowed with more than a day's growth of beard. Even still, he was the sexiest man she knew.

Without asking, he sprawled in the small wooden chair on the opposite side of her desk. "What do you want from me?" The weary question buried her beneath a pile of guilt.

One reason she had felt so entirely miserable since he'd left town was that most of this wasn't Ethan's fault. He had asked her to sit down with him at the diner. That much was true. It was Aria who had invited him home on a cold winter's night. She had been the one to offer him champagne and then proposition him.

She swallowed against a dry throat. "I don't want anything at all. You made your feelings perfectly clear."

"You didn't give me much wiggle room," he grumbled. "You wanted the promise of a relationship in exchange for sex. I wasn't prepared for that. So I bobbled the conversation."

"You make it sound like I was trying to manipulate you. I'm sorry if I backed you into a corner. In my defense, you're pretty good in the sack."

His black frown had her moving the chair backward another six inches. "Don't do that, Aria."

"Do what?"

"Don't try to be flip about sex. It doesn't suit you."

"That's part of the problem, isn't it? You see me as some innocent young thing who needs to be protected."

"You *are* innocent," he said tersely. "Trust me, I know. Most of the women I've slept with are—" He stopped in midsentence, clearly alarmed by how his argument was sliding off the rails. "Anyway," he said, exhaling slowly, "it's a moot point. I'm merely trying to make sure we can still be friends."

Those pesky tears burned the backs of her eyes again. "I don't think we can. I have plenty of friends. I don't need one more."

He paled. "I didn't want to hurt you." His visible guilt knifed her aching heart. The last thing in the world she needed was for Ethan to feel sorry for her.

She shifted a pile of papers on her desk and glanced deliberately at the clock on the wall. "Don't worry about me. I have plenty of men knocking on my door. You don't even make the list."

Her bitter words revealed more than she intended. Ethan wasn't fooled. When he reached for her hand, she jerked away so hard she almost overturned her chair.

"I thought you might have had time to cool down," he said quietly, his gaze searching hers. "But you're still angry."

Angry? That was one word for it. "I accept your apology," she said, completely ignoring the fact that he hadn't actually said he was sorry for anything. "You're free to get on with your life. Do me a favor and close the door on your way out."

He stood and shoved his hands in the pockets of his dark jeans. The cowboy boots he wore looked as if they had long since been broken in. With his broad shoulders, slim hips and drawling good-old-boy charm, he was the epitome of masculine grace.

At the moment, though, frustration rolled off him in waves. "Our paths are going to cross," he said gruffly. "We need to deal with this. You can't ignore me for the rest of our lives."

Aria's stomach clenched hard. He was right, damn him. The prospect was dismal and depressing. She had to end this before she made a fool of herself. Trying to breathe normally, she stood and summoned a smile, thankful for the piece of furniture between them.

"You're making too much of something that was a blip on my radar. And at the moment, you're embarrassing me by bringing personal matters into my workplace. So please. Pretend we never met at the diner. Or better yet, that we never met at all."

His scowl might have terrified her if she hadn't been frozen inside. "That's really what you want from me? To treat you like a stranger?"

"Yes," she said firmly, her heart splintering into a million tiny pieces that could never be repaired. "That's what I want."

The rest of the day passed in a blur. Aria was thankful, for once, that her workload was heavy at the moment. It helped distract her from rehashing the painful confrontation with Ethan.

Between her normal duties at the TCC in Royal and her involvement in several administrative functions that would overlap with the new facility in Houston, she had very little time to grieve about what she had lost. She had done something stupid, and she had paid the price.

Now it was business as usual.

Unfortunately, no amount of pep talks in the world was going to make her feel better anytime soon. She had known for years that Ethan was not the kind of guy who wanted to settle down. Why had she let herself do something so stupid?

Of all the diners in all the towns in Texas, why did he have to walk into hers?

After work that afternoon, she desperately wanted to go home, climb into bed and have a good cry. Either that, or eat a quart of her favorite ice cream and binge-watch something on TV. Instead, she had to go to her parents' house for dinner. Which meant putting on a happy face.

Raymond and Laura Jensen were wonderful parents. They had given Aria love and support and every financial opportunity. She owed them a great deal. Usually she looked forward to their weekly dinner date.

But tonight, she was exhausted and dispirited. The last thing she wanted was to pretend for two hours that she was okay. She would do it, though, because she didn't want to worry her mom. Her dad was less perceptive, though equally affectionate.

She showed up right on time and was swept into the warm, comforting atmosphere of her childhood home. Her mother's pork loin, roasted potatoes and Texas-style green beans were famous. Her father selected the perfect wine pairing and kept everyone's glass full. Oddly, he seemed tense, particularly after he spilled cabernet on his wife's pristine white linen tablecloth.

Cleaning up after dinner would have been a nice distraction, but the Jensens employed a full-time housekeeper. After the meal was done, the three of them—mom, dad and daughter—adjourned to the formal living room. Laura Jensen believed in observing the social niceties.

After half an hour of chitchat, Aria's mother touched her daughter's hand apologetically and stifled a yawn. "I didn't sleep well last night. I think I'll have an early night. But you and Raymond can finish that bottle of wine."

Aria stood and hugged her mother. "Good night, Mama." When the other woman walked out of the room,

Aria sat back down and frowned at her father. "That was odd. Is she okay?"

Her father avoided her gaze. "I told her I needed to talk to you in private."

"What on earth for?" Aria couldn't imagine a scenario where her mother shouldn't be part of the conversation. Her heart stopped. "Are you sick, Daddy? Is it bad?"

Five

Raymond Jensen leaped to his feet and paced. Six years ago he had given up smoking. Aria knew it was a good bet he wished he had a cigarette now. His body language revealed that he was one huge jittery ball of nerves.

He shot her a look over his shoulder. "My health is perfect."

"Then what's the big secret?"

He looked absolutely petrified and haunted and determined all at the same moment. "I've done a stupid thing."

Welcome to the club, Aria thought with black humor. "Go on."

"About eighteen months ago, I took some money from the company. For personal reasons."

Aria frowned. "But it's *your* company, so what's the big deal?"

"It was a *lot* of money," he said.

"How much?"

"Two-point-five million." His words hung in the air. No adjectives. No explanations. Just an incredibly large number.

She sucked in a shocked breath. "I don't understand, Daddy. Why don't you just put it back?" An amount like that would obviously impact the company's cash flow. Maybe even endanger the bottom line.

"I can't," he said bluntly. "I don't have it."

Suddenly, everything clicked into place with an awful precision. "You gambled it away." It wasn't a question. She could see it in his eyes. The fear. The helplessness. The shame.

Her father had been in counseling almost a decade for a gambling addiction. As far as Aria knew, he hadn't been near a roulette wheel or a poker table or a casino in years.

He nodded slowly, suddenly looking decades older. Haggard. Pitiful. "It was online," he said. "Seemed harmless at first. Before I knew it, I had blown through God knows how much. I've maxed out all my lines of credit at the bank. I could lose everything, baby. This house. The business. Your mother's safety net."

Aria felt sick. "Does she know?"

He shrugged. "I told her I'd had some bad news. Maybe she reads between the lines."

"Why are you telling *me* this?"

He came and kneeled at her feet, his face shining

with hope and supplication. "Because you're the only one who can save us."

"I don't understand."

"Harmon Porter," he said.

She stared at him, confused. Harmon Porter was a ridiculously wealthy man in his midthirties. He had asked out Aria a dozen times over the years. And she had turned him down every time. Harmon was a nice guy, but he wasn't her type.

"You're not making sense, Daddy."

He stood again and resumed his pacing. "I ran into Harmon one afternoon in town. One thing led to another and I ended up confessing to him the corner I was in. A few weeks later, he came up with a solution."

"I can only imagine."

"I think you've misjudged him, Aria. He has a big heart. The man offered to give me the entire amount in cash. As soon as possible."

"In exchange for what?"

Her father had the grace to exhibit shame. Though not as much as he should have. "He'd like to marry you, Aria. Start a family. You know how he came from extremely rocky beginnings. I think he wants the legitimacy that aligning himself with our family could give him."

Her mouth hung open in shock. "You're actually pimping me out in exchange for saving your neck?"

"Watch your language, young lady." Her father scowled. "Of course not. This engagement would be temporary only. It would buy me the time I need to get the money and pay him back."

"And he agreed to this?"

"Of course not. I'm trying to tell you that you don't have to marry him in the end. I only need you to go through the motions. As soon as I have the money in hand, I'll take it to him, and you can tell him you don't think the two of you are well-suited or something like that. Break it off gently."

"How do you propose to get this money?"

His gaze slid away from hers. "I have a few plans up my sleeve."

In other words, he was gambling on his penchant for gambling. "Oh, Daddy," she said. Her world was crumbling around her. Oddly enough, the one person she wanted to talk to about her father's crisis was Ethan.

That was no longer an option. Her heart twisted with a sharp ache of regret.

"You could do worse," her father said. "There's something to be said for stability."

"First you say it's temporary, and now you're planning my future with him. This is insane," she said, feeling the walls close in. "You can't possibly expect me to sacrifice myself for your mistakes." The irony didn't escape her. All she had ever wanted was a man who loved her and would give her a family of her own. In many ways, Harmon fit the bill. He was pleasant-looking and agreeable, though somewhat bland when it came to personality.

Harmon Porter was smart, and he actually had a lot of friends.

But he wasn't Ethan.

Her father was gray, his expression desolate. "If not

for me and your mother, think of the people who would lose their jobs if the company closes."

Guilt was a powerful thing. Enabling an addict was self-destructive. Intellectually, Aria knew all that. But how could she let her mother's life be torn apart? Aside from the financial ruin, the shame would crush Laura Jensen if it became public knowledge that her husband had stolen from his own company and lost every penny.

Aria's throat ached. "I'll have to think about it." As the words left her mouth, she heard them, incredulous. First she had lost Ethan, and now this. Perhaps the soap-opera-like crisis was her own punishment for being stupid enough to think Ethan might change.

She stared at her father, for the first time truly seeing his feet of clay. The man who had taught her how to ride a bicycle and drive a car and had read her storybooks every night of her childhood was a deeply flawed human being.

But he was her father.

He stared at her in silence, his throat working. Finally, he spoke. "Harmon would like an answer quickly. He wants to throw a small party at the club soon to make the announcement. Nothing big. A few friends. Family. That's all."

"So he wants to gloat?"

"The man loves you."

"I'm not sure about that. I get the impression that I'm a challenge to his pride. With as much money as he has, most women say yes when he asks them out. I'm one of the few who has ever turned him down."

Her father bowed up, apparently already trying to rationalize his behavior. "He's trying to be my friend. And yours. Don't make this any harder than it already is."

Tears burned her throat. She stood and found her sweater and purse. "I'm going home, Daddy. We can talk tomorrow."

Outside in the lightly scented night air, she got into her car and rested her head on the steering wheel. She was shaking too much to drive. It wasn't fair. How could her father do this to her? What would her mother say? Would she fight for Aria's freedom?

The fact that Laura Jensen had excused herself tonight spoke volumes. Aria's mother was maternal and kind, but she liked her creature comforts and her position in the community. The specter of bankruptcy would terrify her.

At last, when Aria felt calm enough to be in control on the road, she turned on the engine. For half an hour, she drove aimlessly around Royal. Businesses were closed, except for the restaurants. On street after street, she saw images of the life she had always wanted.

Brightly lit living rooms. Families laughing and eating and watching television. So ordinary. So special.

So out of reach. It was a simple dream, really. But in twenty-eight years she had never made it happen. And Ethan certainly wasn't interested in her vision for the future. He'd made that abundantly clear.

She sighed, needing to talk to someone. But who? She had several friends who would open their doors to her without question and listen to her tale of woe. But Aria was a very private person when it came to her personal life. She'd be too embarrassed to admit how she had acted with Ethan and how her world was now about to implode because of her father's addiction.

So instead, she kept driving and eventually found herself outside Ethan's condo, the place he lived when he wasn't in Houston. A light in the bedroom window told her he was probably home.

With all her heart, she wanted to ring his doorbell and beg him to hold her. If she hadn't tried to alter things between them, that might have been an option. Despite the fact that they were now estranged, she still considered it.

As she watched, a man's silhouette passed in front of the window. It was Ethan, of course. She eased the car into a parking space and shut off the engine. She was desperate for advice.

All she had to do was set aside her pride and ask him to help her find a way out of this mess. He was a man with vast and varied resources at his disposal. And he was incredibly smart. Surely Ethan could help her navigate this storm.

Her hands gripped the steering wheel until her fingers ached. It took everything she had to resist temptation. The moment of self-revelation was both stunning and shameful. She wasn't here to get help with her father's crisis. Well, okay, maybe that was the purported reason.

But what had drawn her to this particular street on this particular night was a deep, yearning hunger for the man who wasn't hers. If she went upstairs on the pretext of asking for Ethan's help, she would wind up in his bed.

Suddenly, she had an inkling of what it must be like for her father when it came to gambling. Even knowing that Ethan was bad for her, she wanted him, anyway. Even knowing that a choice to sleep with Ethan meant deep personal harm, she wanted him, anyway. In no time at all, she had become addicted to his touch, his body, his lovemaking.

Her throat ached with unshed tears.

How could she blame her father for his weakness when her own was so immensely foolhardy?

She was close to breaking down completely. Exhaustion. Stress. Fear. All those feelings and more nearly sent her into the very trap she was trying to avoid.

Ethan didn't care about her in any significant way.

And she cared about him *too* much. Did she really want to have her heart broken?

At last, she reached for the ignition and started the engine.

Aria couldn't believe she was actually about to have lunch with Harmon Porter in a private room at the Texas Cattleman's Club.

Though Aria had begged her father to go with her, Raymond had insisted that Harmon would be displeased to have a third party present. So Aria went on her own.

It was a Saturday. Her day off. Normally, she would be spending the morning with friends. Perhaps having brunch or shopping. Something fun.

Instead, she was about to sign her life away.

It would have been easier, perhaps, if Harmon had been an outright scoundrel. She wanted to hate him for his part in this fiasco. Unfortunately, the heir to Porter Worldwide was not an evil man. His father, the CEO, had indulged him and spoiled him and told him he could have anything he wanted if he set his sights on the prize and never gave up.

From some parents, that advice might be golden. In this situation, it meant that Harmon was determined to make Aria his no matter how many times she had turned him down over the years.

Now, because of circumstances beyond Aria's control, Harmon's inflated ego was about to be rewarded.

When she walked through the door into the small room, she saw a table set for two with fine china and all the accoutrements. Harmon was standing. The man with the sandy hair and weak chin held out his hand, perhaps knowing he dared not press his luck at this moment with a kiss or embrace.

"Aria," he said, a shade too heartily. "Thank you for coming. I've been looking forward to this."

To his credit, the smile seemed genuine. Aria fought off the urge to flee. Instead, she shook his hand. "Hello, Harmon."

Fortunately, her self-important suitor liked to talk about himself. A lot. Once they were seated, he dominated the conversation for the next half hour. All that was required of Aria was to nod and murmur her assent from time to time.

Her father had surmised that Harmon wanted to legitimize himself with a tie to the Jensen family. But that seemed unlikely. The Porters were equally prestigious in Royal society.

Aria *knew* why Harmon wanted this deal. He thrived on a challenge. Aria had hurt his pride by turning him down time and again. Now he played this game with a definite advantage. The woman he wanted was trying to make up for her father's failings.

She tried to look at the situation objectively. It appeared that she was a one-man woman. And that one man had stomped her heart into the dust. If she couldn't have Ethan, was any part of her dream salvageable?

What if she said yes to Harmon? His worst failing was his ego. That didn't necessarily mean he was destined to be a wretched husband.

If she saved her father—of her own free will—would having children and a home ever make up for the fact that Ethan was beyond her reach? Or would her father somehow recoup his losses and release her from this impossible situation? Remembering Ethan's cold words after their night together tipped the scales.

At last, the meal wound to a close. Discreet servers had been in and out of the room half a dozen times to take care of any and every need. Harmon barely acknowledged them. Aria was afraid her apologetic smiles did little to make up for *his* rude superiority.

When the dessert was done and they were alone once more, Harmon leaned forward. This time his smile extended to his eyes. "Do you have an answer for me, Aria?"

Here it was. The moment of truth. "I'll marry you," she said quietly. This was her choice. A woman could always change her tune later. Until they stood in front of a judge or a minister, she still had time to ponder her future.

He spoke confidently. "We'll need to get a ring."

Aria was ready for that one. "If you don't mind," she said, attempting to placate him, "I'd rather just have a wedding band."

His face fell. "I wanted to have a party very soon to make the announcement."

Her uncertainty deepened. She swallowed. "We can do that, of course. The ring isn't necessary."

"I suppose not." He paused, clearly thinking. "If you'll give me your guest list, my father's assistant will make the arrangements."

Again, Aria backpedaled. "Why don't we let this one be just your friends and family? It will be more intimate that way. And later, we'll do it again for my side."

Apparently, she had read him well. He preened. "Two parties? I can't quibble with that. I want the whole world to know that Aria Jensen is going to be my bride."

There it was. The arrogance. The need to show off. He didn't even make a pretense of saying anything about love or tender feelings.

She swallowed her misgivings. Despite her father's terrible fall from grace, Aria didn't *have* to do this. She could still walk away.

But could she live with the consequences? So many people would be hurt. So very many… And besides, this was a chance for her to build the life she had always wanted.

She stood up abruptly, no longer able to keep her composure. "I should go," she said.

Harmon stood, as well. His gaze narrowed. "We'll seal our deal with a kiss."

Her throat hurt. Her stomach churned. "Of course."

When he put his hands on her shoulders, it was all she could do not to flinch. His lips were cold and wet, and he pressed his mouth too hard against hers. Oddly, the kiss was lacking in passion. Perhaps she was more right than she knew. It was entirely possible that Harmon wanted the trophy wife more than he wanted sex.

After all, he had enough money to buy as many bed partners as he wanted.

He shook her gently. "Kiss me back, Aria. So I know you mean it."

She moved her lips enough to satisfy him and jerked out of his embrace. That last bit was entirely beyond her control. A woman could only tolerate so much.

Harmon nodded slowly. "I think you and I will get along just fine."

She straightened her spine and kept her expression impassive. Inside, her heart cried out. She wanted Ethan. But he didn't want her. Plan B would have to do. Though she felt bereft, she'd be damned if she'd let Harmon see her pain.

"Thank you for the lunch," she said quietly. "Text me the date and time of the party, and I'll be there."

Six

The morning after Aria's lunch with Harmon Porter, the entire two-point-five million dollars was deposited into her father's bank account.

At first, it stunned her that Harmon wouldn't have made her sign some kind of document. And then she realized the truth. He had no doubts that she would renege on their bargain. Not when her parents' entire livelihood and the survival of their company were on the line.

Layered on top of her misery was the knowledge that Ethan must already be back in Houston. The groundbreaking soiree for the new Texas Cattleman's Club was slated to happen very soon. Ethan would be neckdeep in details at the site. After all, as he had pointed out, no one got ahead in this world without total focus and commitment.

She missed him desperately, but he had been very clear about what he wanted and didn't want.

So where did that leave Aria? Was she a dutiful daughter doing what she must, or a fool throwing away her future? Maybe both.

Harmon didn't waste any time scheduling the engagement party. His underlings must have worked like fiends.

Six days after her private lunch with the man, Aria found herself ascending the front steps of the Cattleman's Club, flanked on either side by her parents. Her father had talked too loudly and too jovially all the way from the house to the TCC, pointing out what a great guy Harmon was and how wonderful it was for Raymond Jensen to know that his one and only daughter would have financial security.

As far as Aria could tell, her father had given up the fiction that he might be able to recoup his losses and put a stop to all this. Or maybe he had tried and then compounded his losses. Maybe he sensed that Aria was looking at the benefits of this alliance and was going to make the best of things.

Her mother was mostly silent, but when she did speak, it was a pretense, as if she truly believed this uneasy union between Aria and Harmon was a love match.

Aria linked her arms in her mother's. She loved her mother, but Aria herself would never be the delicate flower that Laura Jensen was.

When they reached the ballroom, Aria's stomach rebelled. "You two go on in," she said. "I need to visit the ladies' room."

Her forehead was damp with sweat, and she couldn't stop shaking.

In a small act of defiance, she had worn a dress she hated. It had been an impulse purchase off a clearance rack at Neiman Marcus, and couldn't be returned. The pale gold sequins and mostly bare bodice made her look like a dead Egyptian queen.

In the washroom, she ran a damp paper towel over the back of her neck and told herself she wasn't going to throw up. She wanted so badly to call Ethan and beg him for help. Even hearing his voice would be enough. As a child, she had never had to worry about bullies like Harmon Porter. Ethan had always protected her. But now she was on her own.

After five minutes or so, she was only a fraction calmer, but she knew she couldn't hide forever.

When she opened the restroom door and stepped into the hall, a large male hand gripped her arm and urged her around a corner into a shadowy alcove that housed two large janitorial closets.

Her heart stumbled in surprise and joy despite the circumstances. "Ethan? What are you doing here? You're supposed to be in Houston."

Jerking open one of the doors, he glanced left and right, then ushered her into the cramped space. They were so close her breasts brushed his chest.

His glare could have melted the metal shelving behind them. "Is it true?" he demanded. "Are you marrying Harmon Porter?"

Heat radiated from his big, taut body. His outrage was ridiculous. "Yes," she said, lifting her chin, hoping to wound him. "Yes, I am." After all, Ethan didn't want her.

"You don't love him." It was a statement, not a question.

"Perhaps I don't. But he can give me the life I've always dreamed of having. A home and family of my own. As many babies as I want. Roots. Emotional security."

"You can't be serious. You'd go from my bed to his so damn quickly?" Some of his agitation stilled as he searched her face. "There has to be something else going on."

He was perceptive. Aria lifted her chin. "Harmon and I have come to an arrangement. He wants a wife. I want a husband. And Harmon is willing to take care of my father's gambling debts."

"Raymond is gambling again?"

"To the tune of two and a half million."

Ethan cursed under his breath. "Damn it, that's not your problem, baby. Don't enable him."

"Easy for you to say," she muttered bitterly. "I won't stand by and watch the company go under. I have my mother to consider…and all the employees. My decision has been made. I'm creating a future for myself and for my family. Besides, I…"

Ethan was too close. Too warm. Too everything. She had tried so hard to be strong, but being with him like this tore apart her fragile composure. When she couldn't form the words, she simply bowed her head.

The tears came in earnest, rolling silently down her

cheeks and wetting his shirt and tie when he pulled her close.

He groaned aloud. "Ah, hell, honey. I'd like to punch your dad right in the face and tell him a thing or two."

After only a few seconds, Aria made herself step back. She wiped her cheeks with the back of her hand, careful not to ruin her makeup. "I have to go," she said dully. "They're waiting on me to start the party."

His gaze was incredulous. "You can't be serious. Don't do this, Aria. It's beyond foolish. It's almost criminal."

She swallowed hard. "My father could go to prison. He and my mother will lose the house, the business. Everything. I can't let that happen to them. Besides, if Daddy can come up with the money soon, he'll give it back to Harmon, and I'll be free."

"You can't be that naive."

The sharp note in his voice scraped her raw. "You have no right to judge my decisions, no right at all," she cried.

"You could marry me," Ethan muttered, unable to control the words that spilled from his mouth so astonishingly.

He should have been on a plane to Houston. But four hours ago, outside this very building, he'd overheard a conversation in the parking lot that had chilled his blood.

Gossip, of course, though it had the ring of truth.

He'd put his plane ticket on hold, gone home to

shower and change into dinner clothes and raced back to intercept Aria.

She scowled at him. "That's not funny. Let me out of here."

The words he hadn't meant to say hung in the air between them. His mouth was dry. "Is it really two-and-a-half-million dollars?"

"Yes. Daddy hasn't been near a casino in years…not since he finished therapy. But recently, he discovered online gambling. The amount he lost grew bigger and bigger, and he got scared. Then one afternoon, strictly by chance, Daddy ran into Harmon and told him what happened. Harmon offered to give Dad the money if I would marry him."

"Bastard."

"At least Harmon wants children, and he's willing to put a ring on my finger."

The retort was short and sharp and intended to wound. It hit its mark. Ethan flinched inwardly, but kept his expression stoic.

"So am I," he said quietly. "Well, not the kid part. And probably not the marriage. But I *am* willing to be your temporary fiancé. And I'm willing to pay back every cent that slimy opportunist gave your father in exchange for buying himself a bride."

Suddenly, it was so quiet in the narrow closet he could hear the sound of her breathing. It was uneven at best. The smell of industrial-strength lemon polish hung in the air.

Aria exhaled on a shuddering breath. "Why would you do that?"

Of all the answers he could have given her, none was as dangerous as the truth. But he said it, anyway. "I care about you, Aria. I always have. I couldn't live with myself if I let this travesty of a marriage happen. Getting engaged to me will buy you time to find the man you really want to settle down with. It can't be Harmon. It can't."

There was more. A lot more. But that would do for now.

She put a hand on his sleeve. Not provocatively. But almost as if her legs wouldn't support her. "What would you get out of this?"

This part was easy, though her touch distracted him. "You know that my mother remarried after she divorced my dad."

"Yes, of course. I've met your stepfather several times at charity events. He and your mother give generously to the club every year. He's a wonderful man, and he clearly loves her very much."

"I agree completely. Unfortunately for me, the two of them are currently obsessed with the fact that I'm single and not on the way to giving them grandchildren to spoil."

"What does that have to do with me?"

"They're going to be at the ground-breaking party in Houston next week. It would help my case if I could introduce you as my fiancée. My mother had a crappy life when I was a kid. I couldn't do anything about it then, but I can now. I want to make her happy."

"And what happens after the party?"

He shifted from one foot to the other. Being so close

to Aria made it hard to focus. "We'll worry about that later. The important thing is that you won't be tied to that jerk Porter any longer. Excuse me for a moment." He pulled his cell phone from his pocket and pecked out a rapid text. As soon as he hit Send, a wave of relief flooded his chest.

Aria was pale, her gaze troubled. "I can't let you do this. You'd never get your money back. At least I don't think so."

"Your father can give me shares of the company. We'll work something out." He paused, then let himself touch her again. He cupped her neck gently in two hands, feeling how fragile she was. Her hair was up in some fancy knot. It took everything he had not to rip out the pins and winnow his fingers through the golden silk. "Do you trust me?"

Long-lashed blue eyes searched his face. She nodded slowly. "I feel guilty. It's too much money."

"Don't feel guilty," he said gruffly. "I would pay twice that amount to save you from a marriage you didn't choose."

She moved closer and rested her cheek on his chest. "Thank you."

Something inside him shifted and stabbed with regret. He was salving his conscience, but he couldn't give her what she really wanted. "Come on," he said. "Let's go find your fiancé and get this over with."

He straightened a strand of Aria's hair and opened the closet. After ascertaining that no one was watching, he took her by the wrist and drew her out into the hallway.

Aria wiggled free of his light hold. "I'll be the one to tell him. I don't want to embarrass him in front of his friends and family, though."

Her courtesy was more than the other man deserved, but Ethan held his tongue. "Whatever you want to do."

The door to the ballroom was closed. Apparently, all the guests were inside. That made the logistics difficult.

Aria dithered, smoothing her hair repeatedly. "If I go in there, I won't get to say what I need to say."

To Ethan's eyes, it appeared as if she was almost in shock. "Call him," he said quietly. "Tell him you've had an emergency. Ask him to step out here and speak to you in private."

She nodded, biting her lip. "Okay." She slipped her cell phone from her tiny evening clutch and hit some numbers. In a low voice, she repeated the script Ethan had created for her. Moments later, Harmon Porter came bursting through the doorway, thankfully alone.

He stared wildly at Aria, then at Ethan, then back at his fiancée. "What the hell is wrong? And why is *he* here?" The two men knew each other by sight, nothing more.

Aria was so pale Ethan was afraid she was going to faint. But the woman was tough. She faced Porter with impeccable manners and posture. "I'm very sorry, Harmon. But I can't marry you. It would be wrong. I realized I had to call a halt to this charade before the party started."

Porter's expression was horrified. "The party has *already* started," he said, his face turning red. "You made a promise. I should have known not to trust a woman whose father has no self-control."

The blatant insult infuriated Ethan. His hands fisted.

Aria shot him a glance. "Don't make it worse," she whispered.

Ethan didn't bother to lower his voice. He stared straight at Porter, giving him an icy glare that made the other man blanch. "With your permission, Aria, I'd like to punch him for disrespecting you."

Aria shook her head wildly. "Oh, no. Don't lay a hand on him. Please."

Porter brushed her aside, his ire now focused on Ethan. "I don't need a girl fighting my battles. I'm not afraid of this *cowboy*." He made the word a slur.

Witnessing Harmon Porter ignore the woman who was supposedly going to be Porter's bride made Ethan see red. The pompous little goat wouldn't know honor or decency if they bit him in the ass.

As much as Ethan wanted the sheer satisfaction of slugging the smarmy little man, he knew it would upset Aria. So he took several deep breaths and backed down. Metaphorically only.

Aria touched Porter's arm. "I'm really sorry, Harmon. Daddy should never have offered me up as a prize. And I should never have agreed. Surely you knew this was a bad idea."

Porter got up in her face, holding her wrist in a loose grip. "You're mistaken, Aria. There's no going back. I won't be humiliated in front of my friends." The way he tried to intimidate his bride-to-be was the tipping point for Ethan.

"Let. Her. Go."

The three words were simple, but Ethan infused them with steel.

Porter's head swiveled. He stared at Ethan, mouth agape, as if incensed that anyone would dare interfere. "Mind your own damn business."

Ethan grabbed the collar of the shorter man's tux and pulled him away from Aria. "It definitely *is* my business," he said, deadly calm. "The reason Aria can't marry you is because she's marrying me."

Porter's face turned an ugly shade of puce as he jerked back and made a show of brushing off his jacket. For a moment, Ethan thought he might actually have a stroke.

But the man gathered his wits and made a visible effort to calm himself. "You misunderstand the situation, Barringer. Aria's father has my money. A lot of it. And I can assure you it's already gone to pay off his gambling debts. So even if he wanted to undo our deal, he can't."

"Perhaps not," Ethan said. "But I can. Your money will be in your account when the banks open in the morning. Sorry to burst your bubble, but you'll have to buy a bride somewhere else."

Porter was literally stunned speechless. It took him several long seconds to process what Ethan was saying. Then his gaze narrowed. "You can't afford that. It will bankrupt you."

Ethan crossed his arms over his chest and grinned. "Not entirely. But hell, Porter, I'd eat peanut-butter sandwiches for a year to save Aria from your clutches. Sorry, man. It's time to concede the field of battle."

At that, Aria covered her mouth. Ethan was pretty sure she had gasped aloud.

Harmon Porter was accustomed to getting what he wanted, *when* he wanted it. His money funded each and every whim. Being thwarted turned him apoplectic with rage. "You'll regret this, Barringer. And she will, too." He glared at Aria. "I guess she's not fit to be my wife after all."

That did it. Ethan's fist shot out and connected with Porter's jaw, dropping the guy with one swift punch.

Ethan rubbed his hand and glanced sheepishly at Aria. "Sorry," he said. "I told myself I wasn't going to do that."

Her smile wobbled, but it was a smile. "You're forgiven."

Porter clambered to his feet and wiped blood from his nose. "You'll both be sorry you crossed me."

"Stay away from Aria *and* her family," Ethan said, injecting the words with warning. "Or I'll have you arrested for stalking. Now go enjoy your party."

With a bitter grimace in response to Ethan's sarcasm, Harmon Porter turned his back and returned to the ballroom. Ethan barely had time to put his arms around Aria and comfort her before her parents appeared, befuddled and upset.

Aria's father was in a panic. "Harmon threw us out. What the hell is going on?"

Aria spoke up first. "I'm not going to marry him, Daddy. Ethan stepped in and put a stop to it. He and I have been seeing each other. We were on the verge of getting engaged when you told me about your crisis."

"Oh, baby." Aria's mother wrung her hands. "I'm so sorry."

"But what about the money?" Raymond Jensen asked.

Ethan sighed inwardly. Even now, Aria's father was more concerned about his own sorry hide than his daughter's happiness. "I've taken care of it, sir. You and I can come to some agreement about repayment. Aria isn't comfortable being a bartered bride, and I agree with her. Now, if you don't mind…" He put his arm around Aria's waist and drew her against his chest. "I have to fly to Houston tonight, and I'd like to say goodbye to my fiancée."

Seven

Even after the fifteen-minute drive to her house, Aria couldn't seem to stop shaking. Delayed reaction, undoubtedly. She still couldn't take it all in. The ordeal was over. She was free.

And it was all thanks to Ethan.

At the moment, she was trying to get warm. Though it was early March, once the sun went down, the nights were still cool. Aria hadn't worn a wrap. The dash from the club to Ethan's fancy truck—the vehicle he kept in Royal—had chilled her.

Ethan noticed everything. When they pulled up in front of her house, he put the vehicle in Park but left it running, pulling her close to warm her. "You do realize that you're half-naked in this dress?" He ran his hands up and down her arms briskly, trying to erase the goose bumps.

She allowed herself the indulgence of his touch for a long, wonderful moment and then pulled away. "I know it's not a flattering dress. That's why I wore it. A silent protest."

He slung an arm over the steering wheel and sat sideways, studying her intently. "Sorry, honey. If you were hoping the dress would make you unattractive to Porter or to anyone, you failed. You look like a gorgeous ice princess. Makes a man want to melt you."

He was succeeding. The rough timbre of his voice scraped across her rattled nerves and turned her bones to mush. She leaned her head against the back of the seat and closed her eyes. "Thank you," she said, her voice tight with tears she didn't want to shed. She hated women who cried at every little bump in the road. *Pull yourself together, Aria.* "Thank you for rescuing me."

When Ethan was silent for far too long, she sneaked a peek at him. His hot gaze made her nipples pebble beneath the bodice of her dress. "Quit staring," she muttered.

"I didn't rescue you," he said firmly. "I did your father a favor. You did nothing wrong. Nothing except having a heart that's far too giving and loving. And if I'm staring, it's because I can't believe you're sitting here beside me. After our last fight I thought we were done."

"But now you've purchased a fake fiancée," she joked, "and you're stuck with me."

He scowled at her. "That's not funny. Any financial transactions are between me and your father. If you don't want to help me, you're free to go. I'm not Harmon Porter, damn it."

In that instant, she saw that she had wounded his pride. Scooting across the bench seat, she laid her head on his shoulder. "I'm sorry," she said. "I was kidding. Don't be mad."

His big warm hand settled on her shoulder. The way his fingers stroked her upper arm made chills race up and down her spine. He sighed. "I could never be mad at you, Aria. At least not for long."

Being this close to him kindled feelings she had tried so hard to ignore. She wanted him. Badly. In every way there was to want a man. Helping him with his charade was going to put her heart in danger. But despite what he said to the contrary, she owed him a huge debt.

Without Ethan's intervention, she would most surely have ended up married to Harmon. Before tonight, she had convinced herself she could learn to live with a less-than-passionate union if it meant getting the children and the home she'd always wanted. This evening, though, Harmon had revealed his true colors. He would have made her life a misery.

"Tell me about the ground-breaking party," she said.

"It's in five days. Not much time. That's why I'm flying back so quickly. Do you think you can get the time off?"

The thought of him leaving brought back memories of their last intimate encounter. She winced inwardly, remembering how much it had hurt to hear that he wasn't interested in forever. "Not a problem," she said lightly. "As executive administrator, the board expects me to oversee and set up mirror functions in Houston of what I do for the club here. I'm supposed to be at the party to mix and mingle."

"I have a three-bedroom condo very close to the site," he said. "You can stay there with me."

She froze, sensing danger. After a moment, she moved back to her own side of the seat. Living with Ethan day in and day out would be a temptation that might be her undoing. He had paid a ridiculous amount of money to save her from a horrible marriage and to secure a temporary fiancée. Did she owe him physical intimacy? More so, could she resist him under those circumstances? Even now, she wanted to beg him to stay one more night and share her bed.

Ethan read her thoughts as if she had spoken them aloud. His face was grim. "Let's get a few things straight. I asked you to pose as my fiancée, not to be my lover. I'm not coercing you into giving me sex, and I don't want you offering sex because you think you somehow *owe* it to me. Are we clear?"

He was furious. She had impugned his honor.

"I thought…" She trailed off, too embarrassed to say it, and yet heartsick at the notion she had ruined things between them.

"You thought what?" His features were carved in stone.

"I thought you wanted me."

For a moment, his face went blank. It was like that night they met at the diner all over again. When she had thrown herself at him later in the evening, and he hadn't responded.

Muttering beneath his breath, he banged his head against the steering wheel. Then he glared at her. "Are you trying to drive me insane?"

She swallowed. "No."

Ethan closed his eyes and scrunched up his face. It seemed like he might have been counting to ten. Or a hundred. Finally, a huge sigh lifted his chest, which then fell on the exhale. "Okay, honey. Here are the ground rules. First and foremost, I want you. I will always want you. But because of this damned kerfuffle with your father and Harmon and the money, I absolutely will *not* put the moves on you. The only way you and I are ever going to end up in bed again is if you want me enough to initiate sex. You'll have to seduce *me*, not the other way around. And you'll have to convince me that it has nothing to do with guilt or obligation—that you want me to take you hard and deep and fast because we're both mad with need for each other." He stopped and dropped his chin to his chest. Then he looked at her again. "Those are my terms."

Ethan's control was fraying. Having Aria here—so close—made him hungry to touch her again, to pull her beneath him and bury himself in her feminine heat. He'd been celibate since they were together.

Work had been hell, but it was more than that. He couldn't bring himself to slake a physical need with some nameless female when all he wanted was the one woman he couldn't—shouldn't—have.

In a way, maybe the two-point-five mil would keep him from doing something morally wrong. He had used the money to save Aria from a stupid ass. How ironically terrible would it be if he himself broke her heart?

The fake engagement had been a spur-of-the-moment idea, a way for Aria to think she was giving him something in return. It was actually a good idea, maybe even a great one. If his mom and stepdad believed he was working on the idea of starting a family, it would pacify them and buy him some time, at the very least.

Later, he could tell them the engagement didn't work out.

What bothered him now was how very much he didn't want to leave Aria, how very much he didn't want to fly back to Houston. One of his defining characteristics was his total devotion to his career, his complete ability to focus on a project until every detail was complete. But not recently.

For the last few weeks in Houston, he'd barely been able to sleep at night. Many days, he'd found his attention wandering during meetings with contractors and suppliers. He'd even forgotten an appointment once and been late to a couple of others.

Only one person was to blame. He carried her scent in his brain. He could swear the feel of her soft skin was imprinted on his fingertips. His bed felt empty when it never had before.

He had always known this could happen. It was the reason he had stayed away from Royal for big chunks of time over the years. Once Aria had crossed the divide from being a funny, adorable kid to a beautiful, desirable young woman, he'd been in trouble. The only option had been to keep a healthy distance between them.

Now he was taking her under his wing and under his roof, because the other choices were unacceptable. Harmon Porter might try to spread malicious gossip about Aria to protect his own reputation. Ethan wanted to be close enough to know if anything went south.

He had spent most of his life protecting Aria from harm. He wouldn't stop now. Even if he was the person most likely to hurt her.

It occurred to him that Aria hadn't made so much as a peep after he gave her his big speech. He rolled his shoulders. "Did I sound like a jackass just then? If so, I'm sorry."

She leaned forward to adjust the heat vent, giving him a tantalizing view of the nape of her neck and the beautifully feminine curve of her spine. The dress she wore plunged almost to her waist in the back.

At last, when she was satisfied with the stream of warm air, she sat up and gave him a faint smile. "You were very clear," she said. "Crystal, in fact. No sex unless I come begging."

His sex tightened. Was she doing that on purpose? Taunting him? Making his gut tighten with hunger? "I should go," he said reluctantly. "I'm on the last flight out."

Her gaze was wistful and perhaps mischievous. "Couldn't you change it?"

There was no doubt now. The little minx was playing with him. Torturing him, truth be told.

"I've already changed it once," he said, trying not to let her see how she affected him.

She frowned. "Why?"

"I heard rumors you were going to marry Porter. I had to find both of you and stop things before he told the whole world you were engaged."

Her eyes widened. "I never meant to cause you so much trouble." Aria put her hand on the door handle. "It's late. You should go. Good night, Ethan."

She had shifted from laughter to angst in the space of a heartbeat. "Wait, stop," he said, grabbing her arm in a firm but gentle grip. "Don't beat yourself up over this. So I changed a flight. It's no big deal."

Her expression was unreadable. "It is to me."

He tightened his jaw, forcing himself to release her. "It's what friends do," he said lightly.

Aria opened her mouth to speak and closed it again, mute.

He cocked his head. "What?"

She wrinkled her nose. "*Are* we friends, Ethan?"

"Friends come in all shapes and sizes." He was trying to reassure her. Or maybe convince himself.

"Why did you have to tell Harmon we're engaged?" she asked quietly, her blue-eyed gaze searching his face. "You could have just repaid the money. Now it's complicated."

"For men like Porter, everything's a competition. He staked a claim. I stole you from him. It had to be that way. Otherwise, he'd still be insisting you were *his* woman, money or no money. Besides, I told you the truth. I do need a short-term fiancée, especially for the party next week. To deflect my mother from trying to marry me off. You're doing me a favor, Aria."

Her smile was wry. "Nice try, Ethan." She stared at him so long the back of his neck began to prickle.

Women were damnably hard to read sometimes, but he was dead certain he knew where Aria's mind had gone at the moment. The sexual tension that swirled around them in the small enclosed space was enough to make his mouth dry and his gut tighten.

He'd told her he wouldn't make a move on her. Because of the money. But that didn't mean he couldn't telegraph his desire. Without moving his body so much as an inch, he looked her over. From her wary blue eyes to her glossy pink lips to the shadowy valley between her breasts. He let her see the full extent of his hunger.

Aria caught her breath. Slowly, she leaned forward. "Thank you, Ethan," she whispered. "Thank you for tonight."

And then she kissed him.

He forced himself not to respond. At first. She had couched this contact in the context of gratitude. He didn't want her thanks.

His hands fisted on his thighs. The urge to take her in his arms was almost overpowering. But he held his pose, letting her do all the work.

If the kiss had been nothing more than a sweet, swift salute of lips to lips, he would have been fine. But seconds into it, Aria muttered something low and urgent and starting kissing him in earnest.

Lightning flashed between them. Her tongue teased his, sliding into his mouth with disarming confidence. Her arms curled around his neck. Her tiny clutch purse fell, unheeded, to the floor of the truck.

That was all the invitation Ethan needed. He slanted his mouth over hers and took the kiss deeper. He had wondered if what happened seven weeks ago had been a fluke. Or an exaggerated memory. Apparently not.

His heart raced in his chest so hard he could barely breathe, much less think clearly. He wanted Aria. Now. His sex ached, hard and ready. Her dress was little barrier at all. He slid one strap down her arm, then palmed her bare breast, thumbing the rigid tip, reveling in the way Aria moaned her pleasure.

He was seconds away from lifting her skirt and taking her right there in the truck when reality intruded. They were parked on a very public street in front of Aria's house. Even worse than that, he had promised himself he wouldn't let her come to him out of gratitude.

Her body gave him every indication that she wanted this as much as he did, but the timing was suspect.

He couldn't take that chance.

Reluctantly, he released her. "I need to go," he said.

Her gaze was cloudy, befuddled.

His hand shook as he straightened her dress and covered her breast. He swallowed hard. "Are you going to be okay?"

She blinked. "What do you mean?"

"Harmon."

"Oh." After a moment, she nodded. "He's angry. I can deal with that."

"I've never heard anything really bad about him, but we embarrassed and infuriated him tonight. Some men can't let a moment like that go without evening the score."

Aria nodded a second time. "I know you're right. I'll be careful, I promise." Then she smiled. "Ethan?"

"What?" Something about the way she looked at him made him uneasy.

"You say you wouldn't be good in a relationship, but I think you're wrong. Yes, you're a workaholic, but when it matters, you show up for the people you love."

The breath left his lungs. There it was again. The trap. The danger. And all because he had stepped in to keep her from marrying Porter.

He had three choices.

He could ignore her comment and just watch her step out of the truck.

He could put a selfish spin on his actions.

Or, more painfully, he could begin his campaign to make her see how wrong it was to paint dreams about the two of them together.

Though the last one was the cruelest, it was likely the most effective.

He leaned back against his door and donned a sardonic smile. "Why do women always do that?" he said, injecting amused tolerance into the words. "So I happened to be in a place to help you out tonight…so what? It doesn't mean we're soul mates. And if we share a bed, it still won't mean we're soul mates. I can't be any clearer than that."

The words threatened to stick in his throat.

He watched as they found their target.

All of the animation and pleasure leached from her face, leaving her expression dull and wounded. She stared at him for so long, he nearly broke. He nearly caved.

Then without a word of accusation or a goodbye, she grabbed her purse, opened the door of the truck and fled.

Eight

Aria leaned back in the plane, her gaze drawn to the Houston skyline out the tiny window. For the last five days she'd buried herself in work. It was the only way to get through the time that followed Ethan's departure for Houston.

She would have called off the plan to stay at his condo but for two things. First of all, she had promised to pose as his fiancée, and second, Harmon was giving her the creeps. He made a point of walking past her office at the club several times a day. Even more irritating, his name had suddenly—and at the last minute—popped up on the guest list for the ground-breaking party. That had to mean something.

He was probably hoping to keep an eye on her interactions with Ethan. As uncomfortable as it was going to be to sleep under Ethan's roof, at least it would legitimize the fiction that she and Ethan were engaged.

The irony was painful.

She and Ethan had not communicated at all since he'd dropped her at her doorstep, except for a tersely worded text about the car service that was about to meet her at the airport.

When her flight from Royal to Houston landed, the driver who picked her up briefed her on her itinerary. He took her to Ethan's building, where the doorman escorted her upstairs, unlocked the condo and showed her to the guest suite.

After an hour and a half, during which she ordered a snack, showered, and changed into her party clothes, the same driver returned to take her to the new TCC site. At first, she had been confused as to how they could have the ground-breaking party right there at the building when the construction was barely underway, much less completed. But Ethan had explained that the original hotel had a small ballroom on the main floor that would remain structurally intact.

Professional decorators had redone the flooring and walls and lighting, but none of that had taken huge amounts of time. The refurbished ballroom would offer tonight's guests a taste of what the new Houston club would look like when it was finished.

Despite a measure of excitement about the day's festivities, Aria was conflicted about the prospect of seeing Ethan again. His casual dismissal of her feelings had left her shaken and hurt. Nevertheless, she had taken great pains with her appearance. If necessary, she would hide behind a smile.

If he was determined to keep their relationship on a superficial level, she would be foolish to push for anything more.

Fortunately, from the moment she arrived at the new club site, she was both swamped with responsibilities and surrounded by people. Her trickiest task would be diverting Sterling Perry and Ryder Currin to opposite corners.

Not one but three different board members had pulled her aside during the past week and warned her how important it would be to keep the two men apart.

Both Sterling and Ryder had been, and continued to be, instrumental in establishing the new TCC Houston. They had both donated huge sums of money to the new club, and it was no secret that both men were vying for control. But only one man could be the president.

About ten years ago, a group of business leaders—former University of Texas frat brothers—had banded together to form a Texas Cattleman's Club branch in the Houston suburbs. But it had gotten off to a rocky start. Ongoing tensions and rivalries, even a sabotage plot against one member's oil refinery that resulted in another's imprisonment, had taken their toll. So by the time the worst tornado in Royal history hit in 2013, the Texas Cattleman's Club outpost in Houston had quietly disbanded.

Now Sterling Perry and Ryder Currin saw their chance to revive the Houston branch right in the heart of the city. But once again, a fierce rivalry was making the launch more difficult than it should be.

Despite the underlying disquiet, the weather had co-operated for such an auspicious occasion. Blue skies and balmy temps combined for the kind of Houston after-noon that tourists loved and natives lived for. The sun, beaming down on the back of Aria's neck, was hot but not unbearable. She had worn her hair up in a knot in hopes of keeping cool.

She stopped by the table near the entrance to the gar-dens, where guests were checking in. A trio of high-school-age young women was checking names off and handing out name tags. Their volunteer hours would look good on college applications. Aria greeted them, thanked them and moved on to the next item on her list. Meanwhile, she scanned the growing crowd for her two VIPs, who had yet to appear.

The ceremonial shovel-in-the-dirt ground-breaking was to take place in the rose garden shortly before five. Then everyone would make their way into the ballroom and enjoy heavy hors d'oeuvres. Even as Aria mixed and mingled, she kept an eye out for Ethan.

Her nerves were jumpy. She told herself it was be-cause he wanted her to put on a show for his parents. That was the least of her worries, though. Far more dif-ficult was the challenge of pretending that she wasn't getting drawn into his orbit. Even knowing she wanted things from him that he wasn't willing to give, she still felt the pull of his sexuality and his masculine charm.

She glanced at her watch. In another ten minutes, she

was going to have to make some phone calls to track down her missing VIPs.

Ryder Currin strolled among the crowds of well-wishers with a wide smile on his face. In fact, he couldn't seem to stop smiling. He had waited for this day a very long time. Finally! A branch of the venerable Texas Cattleman's Club in Houston. And all because he himself had worked his ass off to make it happen. He had lobbied the members of the Royal club long and hard until everyone saw the benefit of extending the group's powerful reach as far as Houston. Not too shabby for a kid who had, once upon a time, been a scrawny, dead-broke, no-account, lowly ranch worker.

He shielded his eyes from the sun with one hand and scanned the throng. His son, Xander, was there in the distance, but the twenty-five-year-old didn't have a date. He was hanging out with a bunch of his guy friends. Ryder had just about given up hope that his son would ever find another real relationship after his fiancée died. Ryder understood grief and loss, but he wanted Xander to be happy again.

With an inward sigh, Ryder let his gaze move on. All the usual suspects were in attendance today. Including one very beautiful female in her late thirties. Noticing the tall, slender woman robbed him of his smile temporarily. Every time he saw Angela Perry, something about her tugged at his heartstrings.

It wasn't attraction. It couldn't be that. For one thing, he was too old for her. At fifty, he was eleven years her senior. Maybe the odd feeling in his gut was nothing more than nostalgia. Years ago, he and Angela's mother had been friends at a time when each of them had badly needed a friend.

He shook off the unsettling thoughts, and after making sure Sterling Perry was nowhere in sight, approached Sterling's eldest daughter. Actually, there were two of them who claimed that title. Fraternal twins. Angela and Melinda. Melinda resembled her sister, except that her hair was wavy.

Angela's was a waterfall of sunshiny silk, straight and stunning. Sterling's daughter was as smart as she was attractive. Her position as Executive VP at Perry Holdings put her in charge of new business development.

Ryder was inordinately drawn to Angela's beauty, wit and charm. He waited until she finished her conversation, then spoke to her. "Hello, Angela. Nice to see you again."

She turned, and her eyes widened the slightest bit. Her cheeks flushed. "Hello, Ryder. You must be elated at how all this has turned out."

He rolled his lips into a rueful smile. "I'm surprised your father allows you to think anyone other than he is responsible for today."

Angela grinned. "I'm my own person. I can see both sides, believe me."

Ryder folded his arms across his chest. "Your mother would be very proud of you if she was alive."

His quiet words affected her visibly. "I miss her a lot. Ten years is a long time, but it seems like yesterday."

"Perhaps you and I could have dinner sometime. Talk

about her. She was very kind to me when I was a kid with nothing to my name." Ryder hadn't meant to invite Angela to dinner. What was he thinking? Sterling Perry would have a coronary. Not that this would be a date. Not at all. But still.

Just as he was prepared to retract the invitation, Angela touched his arm briefly, a fleeting brush of feminine fingertips that he felt even through his jacket sleeve.

"I'd like that," she said, her genuine smile warm and uncomplicated. "Let's circle back to the idea once the craziness settles down."

He squashed his unease. Like most postponed plans, the meal would likely never come about. Probably for the best, he decided, though the depth of his disappointment surprised him.

Minutes before the ceremony was to begin, Aria spotted both Sterling Perry and Ryder Currin in the crowd. She was about to go and greet the two men separately when a deep voice sounded at her shoulder.

"Hello, sweetheart. I've been looking everywhere for you." Ethan pulled her into his arms and gave her an enthusiastic kiss that left her breathless and shaken.

Before she could do more than blink at him in shock, he tucked her against his side and held her firmly. "I want you to say hello to my mother and stepfather, Sarabeth and John Tarwater. Mom, John—this is my fiancée, Aria Jensen."

His mother rolled her eyes. "Don't be absurd, son. I've known this delightful girl for years." She took

Aria's cheeks in her hands, misty-eyed. "But I can't tell you how wonderful it was to hear that I'm finally going to have a daughter-in-law. Ethan was very close-mouthed about all of this. He only told us last night over the phone. I barely slept a wink."

The distinguished older man beside Ethan's mother winked at Aria. "She's telling the truth. You'd have thought it was Christmas Eve. Welcome to the family, my dear."

Sarabeth stepped back, beaming at both men and Aria. "I'm so happy I could burst."

Ethan kissed his mother's cheek. "You deserve to be happy, Mama."

"And when can I expect grandchildren?" She glanced at Aria's waistline, not even trying to conceal her interest.

Aria's face flamed. "Ethan and I are both really busy right now with getting the new club up and running. Our personal life will have to take a back seat for a few months. But that gives us time to plan. It's all good."

The other woman's face fell. "Oh. I was hoping for a June wedding."

Ethan actually blanched. "Mom, it's March. Good grief."

She shrugged, a motion that was eerily similar to her son's way of expressing himself. "You can't fault a mother for hoping."

John Tarwater stepped into the fray. "Let's let these two young folks do their jobs, love. I see Nathan and Amanda Battle over there. Why don't we go say hello?

Besides, it looks like they've staked out a good spot to see the ground-breaking."

As Ethan's parents walked away, Aria tried to put a few inches between herself and Ethan, but he kept an arm around her. She could feel the heat of his body and smell the scent of his shaving cream. He wore a dress Stetson, as did three quarters of the men present. It shaded his face enough that he hadn't worn sunglasses.

When he looked down at her, his dark brown eyes crinkled at the corners. "Alone at last," he teased.

Her heart was beating far too fast as she relived that last kiss. But this was all for show. "I don't have time to put up with your nonsense right now, Ethan Barringer. We've got two alpha dogs about to tear this place apart." She tilted her head at Ryder Currin and Sterling Perry, who were eyeing each other nearby.

He brushed a thumb over her hot cheek. "Not to worry. The board came up with a perfect plan. They've asked me to welcome the group and say a word about the renovation. Then I'll hand fancy shovels to Perry *and* Currin and they'll *both* do the ground-breaking at the exact same moment."

Aria whooshed out a sigh of relief. "That's brilliant." Though professionally she was interested in what was about to happen with the ceremony, she was far more emotionally invested in whether or not Ethan was going to kiss her again. The knowledge that she so very badly wanted him to rattled her composure.

Despite the fact that he was due at the podium in mere moments, Ethan took her chin, tilted it and covered her mouth with his. For a man on the cusp of a major career announcement in an extremely public venue, Ethan seemed to have no qualms about staking a claim.

Maybe it was because his parents were watching. Or maybe he had spotted Harmon Porter in the crowd.

Whatever the reason, the kiss was sizzling and intense. Aria went up on her tiptoes, leaning in to deepen the contact. "Ethan," she whispered.

She felt him shudder, heard his low curse as he gathered her closer with both arms wrapped tightly around her.

It was as if the entire world melted away.

Until someone nearby cleared his throat. Pointedly.

Ethan jerked backward and nearly lost his balance. Several people laughed and cheered. There were a few irreverent comments.

If Ethan's intent had been to prove to his parents that he was happily engaged, he had made his point.

But he might have taken the ruse a bit too far.

Aria wiped a smudge of lipstick from the corner of his mouth. "Go," she said urgently. "It's time."

With a hot, male look that promised their moment wasn't over, he turned and strode through the crush of attendees. His broad shoulders and lanky frame parted the crowd easily.

Both Sterling Perry and Ryder Currin had made their way to the small, temporary podium, their body language guarded and fierce. Ethan stepped in between them and positioned himself in front of the microphone, surveying the assemblage with an engaging smile. "Good evening, friends. And welcome to the site of the Texas Cattleman's Club, Houston."

A roar went up from the crowd.

Ethan smiled and held up his hand. "My name is Ethan Barringer. It is my honor to be in charge of renovating this historic building and restoring her to new and exciting heights. As I look out over this crowd, I see many familiar faces from Royal as well as new friends in Houston. But I'm here to tell you that none of us would be standing on this spot today without these two titans of industry, these two exceptional men, Ryder Currin and Sterling Perry. Let's give them a hand for everything they both have done to make this dream a reality. Thank you, gentlemen, from all of us."

The applause was thunderous. Both Currin and Perry visibly relaxed, and it seemed as if they both began to actually enjoy the ceremony instead of being so caught up in their dislike of each other.

Eventually, Ethan spoke again. "In a moment, the board would like to invite you all to come inside and enjoy refreshments in the newly renovated ballroom. For your safety, we ask that you stay within the confines of the yellow construction tape as you move from here to there."

He paused and reached behind him for two large shovels. The handles were painted gold and gleamed in the sunlight. Each handle had been tied with a huge golden metallic bow.

Perry and Currin hefted the shovels over their heads, inciting more cheers.

Then Ethan quieted the crowd. "Okay, folks. It's

time. On behalf of the Texas Cattleman's Club in Royal, and in anticipation of the Texas Cattleman's Club in Houston, let's get this project officially underway!"

Sterling and Ryder leaned forward with looks of intense concentration. Two shovels struck deep into the soil. Two sizable clumps of Texas dirt came up on the metal blades and were overturned onto the nearby grass.

As more cheers rose from the crowd, Aria managed to catch Ethan's eye. She waved her arm and gave him a thumbs-up. Pride filled her chest. He was so good at what he did. So smart. So professional. So very well-respected by his peers. How could she not lose her heart to him?

Already she felt guilty about deceiving his mother. She hadn't seen that one coming. In the beginning she'd wondered if Ethan might actually be considering marriage. After all, he wasn't getting any younger. It was plausible to believe he might have been serious about the marriage proposal.

But then he had given her that unnecessarily cold speech about his determination to go through life alone and why women shouldn't get stupid ideas.

Even at the time, something about the words hadn't rung true.

Oh, sure. She believed him. She had believed him enough to be hurt by how callously he had disregarded her attempt to point out that he was a decent man who actually had *feelings*. Why did he try so hard to push her away anytime they seemed to draw closer together?

It was almost impossible to imagine a man like Ethan being scared of anything, and yet he sure as heck seemed scared of having a woman fall for him. Though he was plenty happy to get physically close when the moment permitted, his heart was walled off in some rigid box he'd built when his father had turned out to be a womanizing jerk.

As if her thoughts had drawn him to her, suddenly Ethan was at her side.

"How did you do that?" she asked, blinking in surprise.

"Do what?" He grinned, clearly riding high on adrenaline.

Her query was derailed when they were accosted by a trio of lovely blue-eyed blondes. Angela, Melinda and Esme Perry—Sterling's daughters. Roarke, the only son, lived in Dallas and hadn't made the trip. He and his father weren't on the best of terms.

Melinda shook Ethan's hand. "You handled that beautifully. Thank you so much. I was afraid Daddy and Ryder Currin were going to have a duel before it was all over."

As everyone laughed, Ethan waved off their thanks. "It wasn't my idea, but I was happy to help."

Esme smiled at Aria. "And don't think we didn't notice *your* contributions. Everyone's been talking about what a great job the office in Royal did in coordinating the details for today's event. It's a smashing success."

"I appreciate that," Aria said. "But it's not over yet. You won't want to miss the hors d'oeuvres. And, of course, see the ballroom."

"We're headed in there now," Angela said. "Seems like the two of you should kick back and enjoy yourselves."

Nine

Ethan liked the sound of that. When the Perry women walked away, he cupped the back of Aria's neck in one hand. Her nape was warm. "Are you hungry?" he asked.

She cocked her head, as if sensing his ulterior motives. "Not particularly. Why do you ask?"

"I thought you might like to see something upstairs."

"I have it on good authority that we're supposed to stay inside the yellow construction tape."

He rubbed his thumb over her lower lip. "Did anyone ever tell you you have a smart mouth?"

Big blue eyes looked up at him, filled with a million questions he didn't want to answer and a million secrets he couldn't decipher. "Often," she said. "And it's true."

He took her by the wrist. "We'll slip through the

shrubbery to the side entrance. I have a key. No one will see us leave, I swear."

Fortunately, he was able to keep his word. The crowd had mostly dissipated by now, intent on availing themselves of the free food and drinks inside the building. Ethan's and Aria's responsibilities were largely over at this point. One of Houston's premier printers had produced a glossy brochure for each guest that included not only the history of the hotel, but also a proposed timeline for the renovation and an architect's rendering of what the finished Cattleman's Club would look like.

Actually, disappearing from the festivities was even easier than Ethan had anticipated. No one noticed the two of them walking in the opposite direction from the rest of the group.

When they were out of sight, he reached in his pocket for the key, opened the door and held it for Aria to step inside. It took a few moments for their eyes to adjust to the dimly lit interior.

Aria balked at the next part. "I don't want to get into some creepy old elevator," she said.

He punched the button for the top floor. "We've already had them inspected, serviced and completely refurbished. I would never put you in danger. Surely you know that."

It was a short ride. Yet somehow in that moment, time seemed to slow. He looked at Aria in the mirrored wall of the elevator. Her gaze was downcast, as if she was afraid to let him see what she was thinking. She was radiant tonight. Her dress was the perfect blend of casual and celebratory. Sleeveless and knee-length, it showed off her toned arms and beautiful legs. The fabric was ice-blue, spangled with tiny clear beads that formed flower shapes across the fabric.

Though the neckline was entirely modest, the fit molded to her breasts and flattered her feminine figure.

Suddenly, without any overt provocation on her part, he was hard and aching. His plan to show her what an ass he was, what a bad risk as boyfriend and husband material, was on rocky ground.

Aria was his friend. He didn't want to subject her to the worst of his behavior. He wanted to treat her like a princess. But if he did, she might get the wrong idea.

Hell, he didn't even know what he expected himself. Did he only need a smoke screen to keep his mother happy, or was he going to coax more from Aria? Did he want a fake fiancée? A temporary lover? A convenient wife?

The elevator dinged, signaling their arrival.

As they stepped out, he took her elbow. "Be careful here," he cautioned. "Nothing much has been done on this floor at all." Wallpaper peeled in forlorn curls. The carpet was ripped in places. A general air of disrepair hung over the abandoned hotel on this level.

She shot him a look. "So why are you bringing me here?"

"I thought you might like to see the Elysium Suite." He fished yet another key from his pocket and this time opened a set of wooden double doors. At one time the brass handles would have been brightly polished.

Aria sneezed almost immediately, but her gaze was rapt. "Oh, wow. This is incredible."

"I know. The first time I saw it, I starting calling everyone I could think of until I found a relative of the man who constructed the building way back in the thirties. He built this suite specifically for the famous and infamous to have a place to hide out from the world."

Ethan followed her protectively as she roamed the room. Nothing was overtly dangerous, but the space had been unoccupied for a long time. The decor was French, probably mideighteenth century. Lots of brocade and silk and unabashed luxury. Gilt trim. Delicate wood. And mirrors. Lots of mirrors.

Aria sat down on the edge of the high platform bed and shot a look at him over her shoulder. "This looks like a courtesan's boudoir," she joked.

He kept his distance, only now realizing that even an old musty bed was too much temptation with Aria in touching distance. "You might not be far wrong," he said. "The guy told me that one of the regulars here was some Italian lady descended from royalty. She had a lover who owned a vineyard in California. They would meet in Houston several times a year and spend a week in this very hotel. Rumor has it they never left the room."

"Oh."

He stared at her, frowning. "Aren't you going to say something about how romantic that sounds?"

Her nose wrinkled. "And have you toss it back in my face? No thanks."

His stomach clenched. He wanted to be her hero. But he couldn't.

He also wanted to apologize for his callous speech

the last time they were together in Royal, but perhaps it was better to let it stand.

Instead, he paced. He had known this room would appeal to Aria's sense of whimsy, to her love for larger-than-life tales of grand adventure. What he hadn't anticipated was how being in this suite with her would affect *him*.

She stood up and went up the window, staring out at the panoramic view of Houston. "So what will happen to this suite?" She turned and faced him. "Will it be chopped up into smaller boring hotel rooms?"

He shrugged. "Even worse. This entire floor is being ripped out to the studs. There will be suites, yes. But they'll be ultramodern and chic quarters for the president and the chairman of the board."

Her expression was crestfallen. "Well, that sucks."

"Yeah. The next time you come back, Elysium will be nothing but a memory."

Aria turned her back on the view and leaned her back against the glass. She wrapped her arms around herself and stared at him. "Have you ever wanted a woman badly enough to keep her locked in a room for seven days?"

Suddenly, his collar felt tight. And his erection flexed and swelled even more. If he answered truthfully, he would unravel a sequence of events he couldn't control. Instead, he paced the confines of the suite, picking up a gold ashtray here, a crystal vase there. "I like to keep my liaisons short and amicable. Low drama. It's easier that way."

"So you're a coward."

His head shot up, hot, angry words trembling on his lips. There was no mistaking the dare, the challenge in her voice. "Don't mess with me, Aria." He ground his jaw. "This has been a hell of a week."

She levered herself away from the window and crossed to where he stood. "And where do I fall in your neat little equation, Ethan?"

He shoved his hands in his jacket pockets to keep from touching her. He'd sworn that she would have to come to him. That he didn't want her offering sexual favors for the money he had paid to cover her father's gambling debts. But here in this hedonistic suite, the lines were blurred, and he wasn't sure what she wanted.

"We're friends," he muttered. "It's different."

"Friends." She said the word flatly, as if it was an insult.

"Good friends."

The adjective didn't seem to help his case. Aria's eyes—usually sunny with happiness and good humor—sparked with azure fire. "Then why do I always want to see you naked? And vice versa?"

He snapped. A man could only take so much provocation. Scooping her up in his arms, he carried her to the bed. There was no way he was going to make love to her on sheets that hadn't been changed in who knew how long. So he would have to improvise.

His chest heaved. "Tell me to stop, and I will."

Aria's secretive smile would have put the most experienced courtesan to shame. "I won't say that," she said. "I don't want you to stop. But you'll have to make this fast, because somebody downstairs is bound to notice we're missing sooner or later."

Ethan didn't know if it was the suggestive setting or the knowledge that they were both supposed to be somewhere else or simply the fact that he had been aching for her the entire damn day, but he went a little crazy.

Thank God he had a condom in his wallet.

He set Aria on her feet. "Don't move."

He retrieved what he needed and tossed the packet on the bed. Then he cupped Aria's fragile neck in two big hands and tilted it to just the right angle for a deep, satisfying kiss.

Every time he did this, he forgot all the reasons why he needed to stay away. Aria wanted a husband and a family and forever.

All he wanted was her.

Her arms twined around his neck. "We don't have time to get undressed," she panted. "Just lift my skirt."

The way she said it, the picture she painted, made his throat go dry. "That sounds a little desperate, don't you think?" Surely one of them should make the mature, logical decisions.

Somehow, the situation was spiraling out of control. He had intended to bring her up here to this fantasy-laden suite and teach her what a bastard he was. Demonstrate how he could callously disregard her feelings and use her for a momentary roll in the hay, so to speak.

How could he show her what a total loss he was in the boyfriend-and-husband department when she was just as interested in hot, immediate, possibly temporary sex as he was?

His brain shut down when she touched the zipper of his pants. Nimble feminine fingers found their way to his sex and caressed it.

He cursed, the guttural imprecation raw and probably too revealing for his own good.

Aria laughed. The sultry, knowing sound made the hair at his nape stand on end. This was no masculine power play where he was the aggressor and she the innocent. In this luxurious sexual playground, he and Aria were meeting on equal terms.

When she raked his shaft with her fingernails, his mind went blank. His entire body shook with the need to be inside her.

"Wait," he croaked. "Wait a minute." He slid a hand up under her skirt, caressing one firm thigh, until he found the center of her sex. Shoving aside the undies, he entered her with two fingers.

Aria was wet and ready for him. She must have decided he needed her help, because she shimmied up her skirt to her waist. "Hurry, Ethan. Hurry."

Her face was flushed, her lips pink and puffy from his kisses. Her gaze was sleepy-eyed, her pupils dilated. He wanted her so badly in that moment, that the building could have been burning down around them and he might not have noticed.

He leaned past her and grabbed the condom packet, ripping it open with one desperate motion. Two seconds later, his hands were on her bare hips. There were any number of variations to this scenario, but he wanted to see her expression when he took her. "Kneel on the bed facing me," he urged. From there, he lifted her and lowered her onto his erection.

The feel of her body welcoming his was indescribable. "Ethan…" She breathed his name. For a moment, he was sure she was going to say something else. Instead, she closed her eyes and rested her cheek on his shoulder.

He pumped his hips wildly, his fingers gripping her ass. The sex should have been amazing. And it was. From a strictly mechanical standpoint. His body gave the encounter an enthusiastic perfect ten. He came hard and fast, his climax draining him for long moments until his legs went weak and he was forced to rest both of their bodies on the edge of the bed.

But it wasn't his imagination that by closing her eyes, Aria shut him out. He had told her more than once that he wasn't interested in a relationship with feelings.

So she had taken him at his word.

Suddenly, what happened between them felt as tawdry and abandoned as this relic of a lovers' suite.

He released her and went to the bathroom, where he found a hand towel that seemed relatively clean. He returned to the bedroom, gave it to Aria without speaking and then went back to the bathroom to give her some privacy.

When he had straightened his clothes and reentered the bedroom, he found her standing at the window, her expression pensive.

She smiled when she saw him. "We should get back to the party, don't you think?"

"That's it?" He frowned at her.

The smile dimmed. "You can't have it both ways,

"4 for 4" MINI-SURVEY

We are prepared to **REWARD** you with 4 FREE books and Free Gifts for completing our MINI SURVEY!

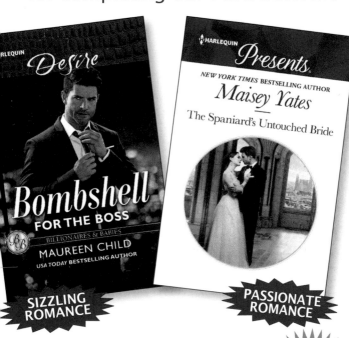

SIZZLING ROMANCE

PASSIONATE ROMANCE

You'll get up to...

4 FREE BOOKS & FREE GIFTS

FREE Value Over $20!

ust for participating in our Mini Survey!

Get Up To 4 Free Books!

Dear Reader,

IT'S A FACT: if you answer 4 quick questions, we'll send you 4 FREE REWARDS from each series you try!

Try **Harlequin® Desire** books featuring heroes who have it all: wealth, status, incredible good looks...everything but the right woman.

Try **Harlequin Presents® Larger-print** books featuring a sensational and sophisticated world of international romance where sinfully tempting heroes ignite passion.

Or **TRY BOTH!**

I'm not kidding you. As a leading publisher of women's fiction, we value your opinions... and your time. That's why we are prepared to reward you handsomely for completing our mini-survey. In fact, we have 4 Free Rewards for you, including 2 free books and 2 free gifts from each series you try!

Thank you for participating in our survey,

Pam Powers

To get your 4 FREE REWARDS:
Complete the survey below and return the insert today to receive up to 4 FREE BOOKS and FREE GIFTS guaranteed!

"4 for 4" MINI-SURVEY

1 Is reading one of your favorite hobbies?
☐ YES ☐ NO

2 Do you prefer to read instead of watch TV?
☐ YES ☐ NO

3 Do you read newspapers and magazines?
☐ YES ☐ NO

4 Do you enjoy trying new book series with FREE BOOKS?
☐ YES ☐ NO

Please send me my Free Rewards, consisting of **2 Free Books from each series I select** and **Free Mystery Gifts**. I understand that I am under no obligation to buy anything, as explained on the back of this card.

☐ **Harlequin® Desire** (225/326 HDL GNWK)
☐ **Harlequin Presents® Larger-print** (176/376 HDL GNWK)
☐ **Try Both** (225/326/176/376 HDL GNSV)

FIRST NAME	LAST NAME

ADDRESS

APT.#	CITY

STATE/PROV.	ZIP/POSTAL CODE

READER SERVICE—Here's how it works:

Ethan. We're playing a game and putting on a show for your family. Don't expect me to do more than that. It's not fair."

Apparently she understood his motives better than he realized. And it made him feel lower than dirt. "Fine," he said, trying not to sound like a sulky teenager. "But when we get downstairs, stay close to me. I saw Harmon lurking around, and he didn't look happy."

Angela Perry nursed her drink and wondered if anyone would notice if she took off her shoes. The stiletto heels were torture, especially after she'd been on her feet all day.

Her heart still beat sluggishly after her encounter with Ryder Currin. He was an incredibly attractive man, and she was definitely interested in getting to know him better. All she did these days was work. Perhaps it was time to give romance another chance.

Her longtime best friend, Tatiana Havery, joined her, looking as fresh as she had this morning at eight. The statuesque redhead had a personality to match her dramatic looks. Since the two of them had been in boarding school together years ago, their lives had taken twists and turns. Tatiana was twice-divorced. Angela had one failed marriage to her credit. Now both of them were VPs at Perry Holdings. Tatiana handled real estate.

Tatiana looked worried. "I saw you talking to Ryder Currin earlier."

Angela lifted a shoulder, feigning unconcern. "So?" she said, feeling her face heat. Everything about Ryder made her itchy. Uncomfortable. In most arenas of her life she was poised and confident. But around Ryder she felt like a self-conscious kid.

It could be the fact that he looked a lot like Brad Pitt and had the same sexy smile. There was something more, though. A gut-level connection. If she was honest with herself, it was a bone-deep sexual attraction. She was pretty sure he felt it, too.

Tatiana chewed her lip. "I've heard rumors about him, chickie. Bad stuff. I think you should stay away from the guy."

Angela burst out laughing. "What do you expect him to do? Lock me in a closet? Sell me into slavery? Don't be so dramatic."

Tatiana was offended. "Fine," she said huffily. "Ignore me. But don't come crying on my shoulder when the truth comes out."

Angela frowned. "The truth about what?"

"I'm not sure. It's just whispers and innuendo so far. But I don't want you to get hurt."

"You're sweet to be concerned about me, but not to worry. I can take care of myself. And besides, Ryder Currin is a stand-up kind of guy. I can't imagine that he has any secrets in his past that would be so terrible."

"You never know. Everyone has secrets. And now that the new club is opening, there will be more people, more crazy, more drama."

"You sound happy about that."

Tatiana's grin was smug. "It's certainly not boring."

Aria's skin smelled like Ethan. Or at least that's the way it seemed to her. Had she really let him make love to her in a deserted hotel room far away from the hustle and bustle of the party and then return as if nothing out of the ordinary had happened?

Three times in the last forty-five minutes, she had tried to slip away from him. And all three times he had tightened his arm around her waist and kept her by his side. Being so close to him was torture. Trying to pretend that sex was no big deal taxed the limits of her acting abilities.

Every time Ethan's mother and stepfather crossed paths with Ethan and Aria at the reception, Ethan nuzzled Aria's neck, or kissed her temple, or tucked her hair behind her ear. His demonstrations of affection—staged for the benefit of onlookers—made her yearn to believe the steamy touches might hold a kernel of truth.

Surely he felt something more for her than friendship and lust.

The evening took an unpleasant turn when Harmon Porter confronted them in a dark corner near the bar. The man—who was several inches shorter than Ethan—had clearly been drinking. He got up in Ethan's face. "I'm having a hard time believing this engagement story, Barringer. There's no ring on Aria's finger. Maybe I'll sue her for breach of promise."

Ethan's expression grew stormy. "Don't press your luck. I kept my part of the bargain. The debt is paid."

"And your fiancée's ring?" Harmon put a hand to his mouth, feigning embarrassed shock. "Oh, my. It's the money, isn't it? You can't afford a flashy stone now that you've cleaned out your accounts to pay me."

When Aria felt Ethan's entire body tense, she put a

hand on his arm and gave Harmon a cool stare. "Not that it's any of your business, but Ethan is giving me an heirloom, a ring that's been in his family for generations. We're having it reset and sized. Now go away and leave us alone."

Harmon's face turned red. He gave them a bitter sneer. But moments later, he turned on his heel and strode away.

Ethan stared after him in disgust. "Stupid toad of a man."

"He has a lot of friends," Aria said.

"I don't care if he's the guy with the cardigans and all the neighbors. The man is a pretentious moron." He glared at her. "I can't believe you were actually going to marry him. What were you thinking?"

Aria's temper rose. "What I choose to do with my life is none of your business."

"You seemed pretty happy about me sticking my nose in your business when he was blackmailing you."

"Not me," Aria said sharply. "My father. And what happened to all your caring, empathetic words about how I hadn't done anything wrong, and I didn't owe you a thing?" She glanced across the room and turned her glare into a saccharine smile. "Oh, by the way, your mother is staring at us."

Ten

Ethan waited a few seconds and then casually looked over his shoulder to see if Aria was right. Bingo. He winced inwardly as he met his mother's eyes.

He turned to Aria. "How about a truce?" he said. "Are you hungry?"

"Actually, I'm starving."

"In that case, come with me." He took her elbow and steered her through the crowd toward the hors d'oeuvres. Once they had added a few items to their plates, they found a small unoccupied table at the edge of the room and snagged it before someone else could sit down. Ethan flagged a waiter and ordered wine from the bar. It was well after six thirty. By all accounts, folks should be heading out for other evening engagements by now. Dinner. Sporting events. The ballet. Opera.

Instead, they seemed to be having far too much fun to leave.

Maybe it was the exceptional appetizers and free alcohol.

Aria gobbled up a fat shrimp with ladylike zeal and licked cocktail sauce from her fingers. "Tell me something, Ethan."

He swallowed a mouthful of chardonnay. "Okay."

"Have you heard anything weird about Ryder Currin tonight?"

"What do you mean?"

She wrinkled her forehead. "Well, when I was working the crowd earlier—before the ground-breaking ceremony—I kept hearing little snippets of conversation about Mr. Currin and how he used to be poor but somehow ended up with this valuable piece of land that made him an oil baron. Do you know anything about that?"

Ethan thought about it for a moment. "It was long before my time, but I do remember hearing that Sterling Perry and Currin once worked on the same ranch many moons ago. Since Sterling is seventy and Ryder is only fifty, Sterling was the foreman, I think, and Currin would have been a ranch hand or something like that."

"So maybe they've always been jealous of each other?"

"But that still doesn't explain how Ryder got rich," Ethan said.

"No. And it doesn't explain all the buzz today, unless people are speculating which of the two men will end up as the president of the new club."

"Well, I have to answer to Sterling in the end, of

course, but he doesn't bother himself too much anymore with day-to-day business operations. Maybe the reason he wants control of the club so badly is that he sees it as a way to stay relevant. Or maybe he wants a new challenge now that the next generation runs most everything at Perry Holdings."

"Them and you," Aria said, swiping another shrimp from his plate.

He swatted her hand. "And me. We all have our own areas of expertise and control. Which seems to work very well for the moment."

"Hasn't it ever struck you as odd that his son didn't want to play a role? If Roarke had stuck around, would you be doing what you're doing?"

"Who knows? Sterling rarely mentions Roarke. They're an odd family. But then again, I guess every family has its skeletons."

"That's a pretty cynical attitude."

"I thought we had agreed on a truce." He chided her with a smile.

Aria held up her hands in the universal gesture of surrender. "I stand corrected." She scanned the room. "So what now?"

"I thought we'd take Mom and John out for a nice leisurely dinner so we can all get to know each other better."

"And then?"

He leaned forward and used the tip of his finger to rescue a tiny drop of cocktail sauce from the edge of her bottom lip. "Then I'm going home with my beautiful houseguest and putting my phone on Do Not Disturb."

* * *

My plan is working beautifully. Who knew it would be so easy to spread a web of lies and half-truths? Though they're not really lies at all, are they? Sterling Perry and Ryder Currin and their families have ruined my life, and they deserve to know the hurt I feel.

After finding that old letter in my father's possessions, I now understand why my life took the turns it did. I hate the Perrys and the Currins for different reasons. They've cheated and stolen things that were mine. Soon, all the dirty secrets will come leaking out like a river of pollution, turning the Texas Cattleman's Club members against both men. At this point, I don't really care about collateral damage.

I want them all to pay. I've had to give up too damn much over the years. There's been too much pain. It's my turn now. And no one is going to stand in my way...

I linger at the back of this fancy ballroom and wish I could go back in time. It isn't fair. I lost so much. My child, my family. My heart will never be the same now that I know the truth.

Royal, Texas. Houston, Texas. When this is all over, everyone will know who I am. Everyone will know what I deserve. And the mighty will fall. You wait and see. It's going to happen. It's only a matter of time.

Aria hadn't expected to enjoy the rest of the evening so much. Having dinner with Sarabeth and John was delightful. For one thing, watching Ethan interact with his mom was illuminating. Mother and son had a tight bond. Aria had known that intellectually, but it had been a long time since she had seen them together like this. And never really since Ethan had been an adult.

She knew the stories about Ethan's father. The man had been charismatic, handsome and, by some accounts, impossible to resist. Apparently, that's the way it had been for Sarabeth. It was only after she had a child that her husband began to show his true colors.

Being cheated on by a spouse was bad enough, but Ethan's father hadn't even bothered to hide his affairs. Not only had the man broken Sarabeth's heart, but he had also humiliated her in front of the whole town.

What was entirely amazing was the fact that Sarabeth had never bad-mouthed her philandering husband to her son. She hadn't wanted to ruin a boy's relationship with his father.

The inevitable eventually happened, though. Ethan's father left for good one day, and he divorced Sarabeth. Even then, she didn't do what most women would have done. She didn't want her son to be crushed by the worst of his father's betrayal. Instead, she told Ethan that she and his father simply couldn't get along. They weren't well-suited. They had made a mistake.

Aria and Ethan had been friends by then. He didn't tell her everything, but he told her enough to make her heart ache for him. She watched a happy, optimistic boy turn into a brooding, deeply hurt young man. Then came the day when Ethan found his mother crying, and he pressed her for the whole truth.

That was the moment Ethan Barringer decided he would never marry and have a family. He had told Aria he was afraid he carried his father's bad genes. If a man could cheat on someone as wonderful as Sarabeth, then there was no hope. Ethan didn't want to take a chance.

Now here they were, almost fifteen years later, and Ethan's emotional shell had only grown thicker and more impervious.

Aria could tell herself she might change him, but what were the odds? She knew he cared about her. And the sex was great. Still, did she want to risk having her self-esteem and her emotional well-being shattered?

At the moment, she and Ethan were sitting hip-to-hip in a wood-and-leather booth with John and Sarabeth on the opposite side. Ethan had wanted to treat everyone to a five-star restaurant. His mother had insisted she was happier at this hole-in-the-wall pizzeria that had flourished in Houston since she was a child. Sarabeth remembered her grandma bringing her here, she claimed, when they visited from Royal.

The booths were small and definitely cozy. Ethan's hard thigh pressed against Aria's leg, distracting her from the conversation. His long arm draped across the back of the seat behind her, hemming her in pleasantly.

Sarabeth beamed at her son and Aria, her face alight with expectation. "So tell me," she said. "How did you two connect after all these years?"

Ethan ran his fingers along Aria's bare upper arm. "You tell her, sweetheart."

Aria pinched his thigh underneath the table. Hard. But she pinned on a smile. "It was entirely by chance. You know, I guess, that Ethan has been making multiple trips back and forth between Houston and Royal to meet with the TCC board and pitch his case for the construction of the new club. The night he won the bid, he was celebrating all alone at the diner. I walked in out of the cold, and that was that."

Sarabeth clasped her hands under her chin. "So romantic. It was meant to be." She gave her son a coy glance. "I told you so."

Aria looked from one to the other. "Am I missing something?"

Ethan's mother grinned. "This dear boy has told me for years that he absolutely is *never* going to get married and settle down with a family."

"No big surprise there." Aria tried to make a joke of it. If she hadn't been sitting so close to Ethan, she might have missed his reaction. But because they were crowded together, she knew the exact moment his entire body tensed at his mother's provocative words.

She tried desperately to think of a way to derail the conversation, but Sarabeth was excited and determined to have her moment. "He's always hated his father for the way he treated me. Even worse, Ethan has been afraid he's too much like this father. That he might hurt the people he loves. That he might cheat on a woman and make her life a misery. So he decided he would keep all of his relationships strictly physical."

Even John tried to intervene, perhaps picking up on Ethan's discomfort. "Sarabeth…"

She waved a hand, discounting the interruption. "I knew my dear sweet boy was wrong. I knew that when the right woman came along, he would fall and fall hard. And I knew that with his honor and his compassion and his bone-deep decency, he would never hurt or betray a woman." She reached across the table and took Ethan's hands in hers. "I love you, son. And I'm so very, very excited and grateful tonight. John has brought joy to my life, but seeing you here with Aria makes my happiness complete."

Ethan cleared his throat, his face flushed with emotion that could have been embarrassment or discomfort or both. "Thank you for believing in me, Mama. I always wanted to make you proud."

"You have. And you will."

Suddenly, Sarabeth turned her maternal instincts on Aria. "And what about you, sweet girl? How do you feel about starting a family?"

"Um, I already told you. We've had to table that idea for the moment. The new Texas Cattleman's Club here in Houston is our baby right now."

Sarabeth wrinkled her nose. "Not very exciting for me."

John pulled his wife close and kissed her cheek. "All evidence to the contrary, my love, the world doesn't revolve around you. I'm sure Aria and Ethan will give you a grandbaby when the time is right."

After that, the pizza arrived and the conversation moved to less personally volatile topics like books and movies. Not surprisingly, there was even a bit of benign gossip about some of the more flamboyant personalities who had attended the ground-breaking ceremonies earlier.

Neither Sarabeth nor John mentioned anything about the rumors Aria had heard about Ryder Currin. Perhaps there was no substance to the hushed whispers, or maybe she had misheard a conversation here and there.

At last, the hour drew late, and Ethan's mother wanted to go back to her room and put up her feet. Aria was surprised the older couple wasn't staying with Ethan, though, of course, she didn't speak her thoughts aloud.

Sarabeth gave her a saucy grin. "A grown man doesn't need his mother hovering. John and I already had reservations at my favorite little boutique hotel, but when I heard you two were newly engaged, I was especially glad John and I weren't intruding."

Ethan kissed her cheek. "You never intrude, Mama."

Outside on the sidewalk, everyone said their goodbyes. Ethan hailed a cab for the older couple. Then he turned to Aria, his expression unreadable. "You ready to go home?"

"Sure."

Ethan had parked two blocks away, an easy walk. They should have had plenty to talk about en route to the car. The ground-breaking. The incredible turnout for the ceremony and the party. The unveiled antagonism between Sterling Perry and Ryder Currin.

Neither of them said a word.

Aria suspected that Ethan was upset about his mother's editorial comments concerning his love life. If he and Aria had actually been wild about each other, the whole incident would probably have been funny. As it was, neither of them was laughing.

The trip back to the condo was mercifully brief at this hour. Ethan turned on the radio to fill the silence.

Once they reached his elegant building, he handed off his keys to a uniformed valet, and they made their way upstairs via a sleek, fast elevator that left Aria's stomach somewhere around the third or fourth floor.

Ethan had the penthouse. Of course. She wondered if he would be able to afford it now that he had covered her father's enormous losses. Once again, she felt the weight of what she owed him.

Surely, given all he had done for her already, it would be cruel and immoral to try to change him. The man had suffered a great deal during his childhood and adolescence. He'd coped the only way he knew how.

Aria wanted him on her terms. Was that incredibly selfish?

Ethan unlocked the door and stood back for her to precede him.

His body language was jerky, his usual masculine grace obviously affected by the emotional exchange of the evening.

She laid her clutch purse on the table in the entryway. "Thank you for letting me stay with you," she said quietly. "This is so much nicer than an impersonal hotel."

He opened a shallow drawer in the table and handed her a set of keys. "Keep these while you're here," he said gruffly.

"Thank you." Her visit would be relatively brief. Ryder Currin was hosting a fund-raising gala for the new club in forty-eight hours. The two social events had been planned close together intentionally, so out-of-town guests could attend both.

After the big party, there would be no reason for

Aria to linger in Houston. Until the club was actually operational, most of her work would be accomplished from Royal.

Ethan's jaw was tight. "I'm sorry to be a poor host, but I have some work to do."

Aria's face flamed. The curt dismissal was shocking. After his comment about putting his phone on Do Not Disturb, she had assumed this evening was headed in a different direction. "Of course," she said. "I'll see you tomorrow." She turned on her heel and fled to her room, her eyes hot with tears.

Eleven

Ethan ripped off his tie and strode toward his office, cursing beneath his breath and telling himself the sharp pain in his chest was indigestion. He'd thought the uncomfortable dinner with his mother was the worst he could feel tonight. Turns out, he was wrong.

He was a cheat and a liar. Because he'd wanted to make his mother happy, he'd created this elaborate charade. And the charade had been birthed out of Aria's crisis with Harmon.

What did that make Ethan? Was he some kind of Machiavellian showman? Manipulating everyone and everything to his will?

He paced the confines of his office, wishing he didn't have a guest, wishing he could go to the gym and beat out his frustrations on a punching bag or on the racquetball court. Seeing the wounded expression in Aria's tear-drenched blue eyes just now was a sight that would live with him forever. She kept expecting him to be a certain kind of man, and he continued to disappoint her.

Knowing she was down the hall made his hands shake and his heart slug in his chest. He poured himself a generous shot of whiskey and then didn't drink it, choosing instead to drop into a deep, leather chair and nurse his grievances along with his untouched alcohol.

He swirled the amber liquid in the cut-glass tumbler and studied the patterns in the bottom of the crystal. Normally, he relished the peace and solitude of his home atop one of Houston's premier downtown skyscrapers. Tonight, even though another person would sleep beneath his roof, he felt inexplicably lonely and bereft.

Hell, he was losing it.

A noise, barely perceptible, had his head jerking up. His hand trembled so badly that several drops of liquid sloshed onto his leg.

He swallowed against a dry throat, wishing he had downed the damn whiskey. "Aria? What are you doing here?"

She had changed out of her party dress and let down her hair. Clearly, she had showered, because her blond tresses were darker than usual. Damp, wavy tendrils clung to her neck and collarbone. She wore a white robe of some silky material that revealed nothing at all and yet managed to make it very clear she was naked underneath.

His sex flexed and hardened, pressing uncomfortably against his zipper. He didn't want to adjust himself for fear of drawing attention to his condition and letting her know what her presence did to him.

When she didn't say anything, he repeated the question. "What are you doing here?"

She entered the room slowly, paused at his desk and picked up a book about economic policies in the European Union. "It doesn't *look* like you're working."

Her voice was husky, mocking him.

"I needed a break. It's been a long day."

"Indeed." Her smile was bland.

Suddenly, he was back in the Elysium Suite with her legs wrapped around his waist. *Holy hell.* "You should go to bed," he said firmly. "It's late."

"Eleven thirty? Do you turn into a pumpkin at midnight? Maybe I should stay and watch."

He clenched his jaw. Sweat beaded his forehead. "I'm not in the mood for this," he said, the words tight with a frustration and longing that he hoped like hell she didn't hear.

Aria tossed aside the book and crossed the thick carpet to where he sat. Her bare feet made no sound at all. When she stood at his knees, she took the glass from his numb fingers, tried a sip and wrinkled her nose. "Ugh. I've never seen the appeal."

"It's a hundred dollars a bottle. Show some respect." The way her silky robe parted around his leg riveted his attention.

Without realizing it, he had clenched his hands on the arms of the chair. His knuckles were white. Aria noticed. Of course.

Her expression softened. "You asked me why I'm here…"

He swallowed. "It doesn't even matter. Just go."

She sat down in his lap. The sides of the robe gaped, revealing a feminine pair of tanned, toned thighs. "I hope you don't mean that," she said. "You told me when you paid my father's debts that I would have to make the first moves when it came to sex. That you didn't want my gratitude or my obligation."

He nodded, trying to pretend he was in control. "I remember."

"I want you, Ethan." She curled an arm around his neck. Her breasts pressed against his chest.

"Aria, I—"

She put two fingers against his lips. "Shhh. Don't say anything. I'm not asking you to change who you are. I'm simply proposing détente for the next few days. Let's enjoy ourselves until the gala is over. I'll go back to Royal after that, and when you think the time is right, you can tell your mother that I broke things off. That way she won't be mad at you, and it will buy you some time before she starts nagging you about a new relationship."

He stroked her back, feeling the warmth of her skin through the slick fabric. "You would do that for me?"

Aria rested her forehead against his. "You're my friend, Ethan." She ran her thumb across his bottom lip. "My very good friend."

How was a man supposed to do the right thing in the face of such temptation? He couldn't even *separate* right from wrong anymore. Up from down. Wanting from needing.

He knew exactly the kind of man Aria wanted, the kind of man she needed. And even knowing that, he was going to take what she was offering without promising anything in return. He could try to salve his conscience by reminding himself that he had saved her from Harmon Porter. That was something, surely.

Then again, it was easy to give money when a man had plenty of it. What Aria wanted was his heart.

He cleared his throat, but the words still came out hoarse. "I don't want to hurt you."

She bit his earlobe, hard enough to sting. "Maybe you should worry about protecting your own heart. Assuming you have one."

She said that last bit with a teasing smile.

He'd used up his final stores of patience. "I told myself I wasn't going to take advantage of you while you were a guest in my home." He made the admission quietly, wanting her to know he had given the situation considerable thought.

"I'm naked. And in your lap. I think you could be excused for touching me now."

Beneath her humor he finally saw the vulnerable heart, the hesitant courage. She wasn't sure of him. Of them.

"You are an amazing woman," he said, winnowing his fingers through her hair, separating strand from strand. "I formally accept your offer of détente."

Her smile widened, became radiant. "What a smart man."

He groaned and pulled her closer still, capturing her mouth in a hungry kiss. She arched into him, her lips parting as he slipped his tongue into the sweet recesses of her mouth. She tasted like toothpaste.

Suddenly he was aware of how fresh and sweet she was and how rumpled he felt. "I need a shower."

"Are you sure?"

Her disappointed pout made him laugh. "You could join me."

"No. My hair's almost dry. But I can warm up your bed."

He blinked, stunned. Had she always been this sure of what she wanted? And if so, why had he stayed away?

Rising to his feet with her in his arms, he held her against his chest, inhaling the scent of warm woman and his own shower soap. "I'll make it quick, I swear."

She ran her fingers along the late-day stubble of his chin. "I *really* hope you're talking about the shower."

He jogged down the hall laughing helplessly, trying not to drop his sexy armful. He never remembered being so incredibly aroused and ridiculously amused at the same time. Aria had that effect on him.

In the doorway to his bedroom, he tried to see his domain through her eyes. The dark woods and masculine colors were nothing out of the ordinary. But when he dropped her on his bed, she looked like an angel on his navy comforter. Well, maybe not *exactly* an angel.

The robe was mostly open now. Only a knot in the narrow sash kept the last of her secrets hidden from him. "Make yourself at home," he said huskily, as he unbuttoned his shirt.

Aria reclined on her elbows and watched him undress, a tiny smile tilting the corners of her perfect pink lips. "You really are a gorgeous man."

His hands stilled on the waistband of his pants. "I'll finish this in the bathroom. Don't move."

Aria's heart was beating so rapidly she felt a little faint. An hour ago, she had been wallowing in despair. Until it finally dawned on her that Ethan had made a huge deal about her coming to him and not the other way around.

After they had returned home from the meal with his parents, she had taken his odd mood as rejection. She'd been deeply hurt and confused. When in fact, Ethan wanted her just as much as she wanted him.

Maybe she was skating along the precipice of self-destruction. But she couldn't draw herself away. Whatever happened, happened. Ethan didn't want forever. He'd made that abundantly clear.

But he wanted tonight, so Aria was going to wallow in these moments and not think about the future.

When he opened the door from the bathroom five minutes later, she literally lost her breath for several long seconds. She tried to smile and speak, but her vocal cords were frozen, and her lower jaw trembled.

Ethan had a towel around his waist. That was the extent of his wardrobe. Because she saw him in business attire so often, she sometimes forgot how wonderfully powerful his body was, how utterly masculine in its raw beauty. His shoulders were wide, his chest lightly dusted with hair.

Where the damp towel clung to his hips, muscles delineated his taut abdomen. His arms hung at his sides, but he wasn't relaxed, because his hands were fisted.

Aria was sitting up against the headboard with her arms linked around her knees. She flipped back the covers with one hand. "Care to join me?"

Ethan's hot, determined stare actually made her shiver. Her thighs clenched. She felt like the proverbial mouse caught in the visual crosshairs of a very hungry cat.

He loosened the simple knot and tossed the towel on the closest chair. Now she could study him from head to toe. His erection reared thick and firm against his belly. A river of emotion swept over her. Want. Need. But not love, not that. She was determined to do this the way a man would.

Light and easy. Enjoy the carnal bliss. Take pleasure in the moment.

Ethan climbed into bed and dragged her into his arms. His skin was still damp, but hot. Oh, so hot. It was a wonder steam didn't rise up from the two of them.

"Well, this is different," he drawled, nuzzling her neck.

"What do you mean?" she croaked. It was difficult to string words together in a coherent sentence. Ethan's naked body was a feast for the senses, and at this particular moment, her senses were on overload.

"Doing it in a bed," he chuckled. "Maybe third time's a charm."

"I never knew you were so conventional."

Ethan grabbed a hank of her hair and tilted her head

so he could nibble the sensitive spot just below her ear. "And I never knew how easily you could make me lose control. I'm not sure I like it."

She found his sex beneath the covers and wrapped her hand around it. "If you want an apology from me, big guy, you're going to have to wait a very long time. I like driving you crazy."

He reared up on one elbow and gave her a hooded smile. His unoccupied hand caressed her breast and nipple, making her moan aloud in an embarrassing fashion. "I'm beginning to see that," he said.

Vulnerability choked her. She closed her eyes, not wanting him to see everything she was feeling in that moment. Actually, she didn't *want* to feel what she was feeling. Doggedly, she shoved aside every yearning, heartbreaking, bound-to-be-unfulfilled wish and concentrated on the physical pleasure that cascaded through her limbs.

Ethan's big hands on her body created magic and chaos wherever he touched her. Tenderness and demand. Hunger and gentleness. Despite the relative newness of their physical relationship, he seemed to know intuitively which strokes, which caresses, gave her the most pleasure.

The first climax caught her by surprise, hot and sharp. He held her close and played with a strand of her hair until her breathing stilled. Then he drove her up again. Each time she tried to touch him intimately, he moved her hand, as if determined to be the one in control of this encounter.

Only when a second orgasm left her weak and spent

did he roll over, grab a condom and, moments later, move between her thighs.

"Wait." She thrust a hand, palm flat against his chest.

Ethan's pained expression was incredulous. His face was flushed, all sharp angles and taut skin. "What?"

She looked up at him, trying to find answers in his bittersweet-chocolate eyes. "We may be temporary, Ethan. But I won't let you call all the shots. We do this on an equal footing or not at all."

The flicker of his eyelashes told her she had hit on at least a shred of truth. Ethan didn't want to move past a certain level of intimacy.

Sex came in all kinds of shapes and sizes. Every time a man and a woman came together, the possibility existed that a connection was being forged, strengthened.

But Ethan didn't want to be bound to anyone.

The standoff she hadn't intended to initiate seemed to last forever. Finally, a huge shudder wracked his big frame as he cursed and flopped onto his back. "Fine," he said gruffly. "I'm not in charge. I'm all yours."

That last bit wasn't exactly true, but she wasn't inclined to quibble over semantics now that she had gotten her way.

Twice now, Ethan had coaxed her into a firestorm of incredible pleasure. She wanted to return the favor. But even more than that, she wanted to show him, without words, how much he meant to her.

He might not want to listen to her talk about romance and love and forever, but she could at least give him a taste of what he would be missing when he decided they were done.

Despite his apparent compliance, his fingers were clenched in the sheets. She wanted to smile, but she didn't dare.

Instead, she removed the unused protection, so she could caress his sex skin to skin. His shaft was thick and long. The slit at the crown oozed fluid. When she rubbed it with her fingertip, his body quaked.

"Aria," he said, the word like sandpaper.

She leaned over and kissed his nose, his chin, his mouth, long and deep. "Yes, Ethan?"

He bit her bottom lip, not as passive and compliant as he appeared. "I want to be inside you when I come. Don't fool around too long."

"I have faith in you," she said. "I think you can hold out."

His eyes closed, the lashes ridiculously long and thick for such a masculine man. "I never knew you had a sadistic streak." The wryly muttered words made her determined to play the game until the end.

She cupped his sac in her hand and squeezed gently, monitoring the emotions that contorted his features. He was breathing like a distance runner, his chest heaving.

Carefully, she spread his legs and moved between them, kneeling and leaning forward over him so that her breasts brushed his chest. She put her hands on his shoulders. "Look at me, cowboy."

When his lashes finally lifted, the searing expression in his eyes made her own sex clench and ache despite her recent abandon. He gripped her butt. "I want you, darlin'."

She leaned down and kissed him recklessly. "Soon,"

she promised. "Soon." Rubbing her body against his, she gave him everything he wanted except penetration. When he caught a nipple between sharp teeth and tugged, she cried out, momentarily sidetracked.

Pleasure shot from her breast straight to her womb. Suddenly, her patience eroded. "I'm ready," she said. "Hurry."

His feral grin mocked her about-face, but she didn't care.

He tumbled her aside and reached toward the bedside table.

Twelve

Ethan yanked open the drawer. "Damn it." Desperately, he rifled through the pile of TV remotes and old batteries and paperback novels.

Aria leaned her chin on his shoulder. "What's wrong?"

"That was the last condom. And it tore when you took it off."

"Oh." The disappointment in her voice was a mere fraction of what he was feeling.

"I'll check the bathroom."

His erection hurt like a toothache. He hobbled to the other room and started yanking open drawers and cabinets. Dental floss and shaving cream and Band-Aids, but no condoms.

Frustration pounded in his veins. This couldn't be happening.

Aria appeared in the doorway—all slender, pink-and-white and naked. "Can I help?"

He couldn't even look at her. "Go back to bed."

"You really don't have any?"

He had his back to her. Their gazes met in the mirror, his hot and angry, hers abashed and unsure.

"No," he said curtly. "Apparently that was the last one."

"I thought sexually active men bought those by the dozens."

"The amount of actual working knowledge you have about men could probably fit in a shot glass," he snarled.

Aria lifted her chin. "I know enough to realize that when they don't get…*satisfied*, they turn into rude Neanderthals."

She had him there. He turned around and exhaled, dropping his chin to his chest. "I'm sorry. You should go to your room, I think."

"Why?"

She couldn't be that clueless. "I can't make love to you without a condom. I won't take the chance of getting you pregnant."

"Of course not," she said, her eyebrows drawn together in a cute little frown. "But there are other ways."

His erection hadn't subsided at all during this conversation, but now it bobbed eagerly. He cleared his throat. "I'm listening."

"I'm cold," she said. "We can discuss this underneath the covers."

He followed her to the bed, though he stopped short

of climbing in with her. Given his current state of mind, his self-control was iffy. "It's seventy degrees in here."

"Maybe I'm nervous." She had the covers pulled up to her chin.

"Are you?" he asked. It seemed impossible after all that they had shared up until this point.

"Of course I'm nervous, you big, gorgeous testosterone-laden dummy. I'm trying to keep this evening from fizzling out, and you're not helping me."

Her indignation made him smile, despite his physical discomfort. He sat on the edge of the bed and took her hand in his. "I'm sorry. I'm sorry I said you were clueless about men. That was kind of mean."

She sniffed. "Yes, it was."

"So what is this idea that's keeping you here instead of going back to your room?"

"Well, um…" She flushed a rosy pink all the way from the tops of her breasts up her throat to her face and into her hairline. "I've heard that men like to… Well, or fantasize about, um…"

He tipped up her chin. Those amazing Aegean-blue eyes were filled with what seemed to be a combination of excitement and mortification. "Just say it, Aria. What are you trying to say?"

Her throat moved as she swallowed hard. "I thought since you've already made me come twice, and since you don't have any more condoms, that you might like to, um…pleasure yourself on my breasts."

His head exploded. At least that's how it seemed. Her words were a shock wave that reverberated inside his brain and left him paralyzed. Did she have any clue what she was proposing?

He dropped her hand and stood up, wishing he was wearing a robe. And then it occurred to him that he didn't even own a robe. He lived in Texas, for God's sake. And he was babbling. Internally, but still.

Aria stared at him with big eyes. "Ethan?"

"I'm thinking," he muttered. He was thinking that of all the amorous activities he'd ever engaged in with a variety of women over the years, that particular thing hadn't been one of them. Somehow it seemed either extraordinarily private and special, or maybe the total opposite—disrespectful.

Hell. Aria was tying him up in knots. He'd been hard for about a million years now, and this was the fork in the road.

Choice A? He sent her away to her own bedroom and he spent a very restless, uncomfortable night, no matter whether he took matters into his own hands or not.

Choice B? He accepted Aria's invitation and waded deeper into waters of intimacy with this extraordinary woman, a woman he was determined to keep at a safe emotional distance.

She sat up, allowing the sheet to slide away, exposing her breasts. "Have I shocked you? Am I being unladylike? You didn't even want me to touch you earlier tonight, so perhaps I stepped way over the line just now."

"Don't say that," he snapped. It hurt To look at her.

"Then you explain to me why you're still standing over there."

He opened his mouth and closed it. "I don't need you to…" He trailed off, his chest heaving.

She lifted an eyebrow, staring at his erection. "You need *something*. Look at that poor guy. He's been waiting for hours."

The hint of humor restored his equilibrium. "He'll get over it. He's resilient."

Aria frowned. "Am I way off base here? What's the big deal?"

The big deal was a very big deal. It was one thing to come inside a woman when both of you were carried away in the throes of lust and passion. It was another situation entirely to have a woman watch something as intensely personal as a man ejaculating on her breasts.

His chest heaved. His entire body began to tremble. He wanted Aria. And he couldn't have her. Not in that way. Not tonight. But he also dared to want what she offered in the meantime.

The notion was deeply disturbing and wildly exciting, which was enough to give him pause. Was he getting in too deep?

She held out her hand. "Come to bed," she cajoled. "Please, Ethan."

He couldn't evict her from his bed if he tried. And he couldn't walk away. He didn't want to…at all.

Swallowing his misgivings, he nodded jerkily. Before he could take more than a single step toward the bed, Aria tossed back the covers and spread her legs. Her smile was open. Uncomplicated. Loving.

That last one should have alarmed the hell out of

him. It should have set off all the warning bells. But he was too far gone.

He kneeled on the mattress and kissed her ankle, chuckling when she protested. "Ticklish, are we?"

She grabbed his hair. "Yes…" The word ended on a sigh.

Her smooth thigh beckoned. He worked his way up from her ankle to her calf to her knee and finally to the mother lode, where he parted her sex with the tip of his tongue.

Aria moved restlessly. "I can't," she said. "Not again."

"You underestimate yourself, sweetheart. Or maybe you underestimate me."

In minutes he had her trembling and panting and crying out his name as he sent her over the edge a third time.

Her sensuality struck deep in his gut. He loved giving her pleasure. He loved watching her face as she came apart in his arms.

He loved her.

No. No, he didn't. Or if he did, it was affection. Born out of a years-long friendship between them both.

Her breathing slowed at last, and she opened her eyes. "Wow. You're really good at that."

He shrugged. "I like watching you. It turns me on."

Her mouth fell open in a little O of surprise, as if she couldn't believe he would be so honest. She nodded slowly, her gaze drifting to his sex. He was so hard he wondered if he'd ever be *not* hard again. Wanting her was a living, breathing force inside him.

He was desperate to be inside her. Aching. Wanting to possess her completely. But he wouldn't take chances.

So he would take the incredible gift she offered him. "Are you sure?"

She didn't pretend to misunderstand. "I am. With one caveat."

His stomach clenched. "And that would be?"

For once, there was no smile on her face at all. No teasing. Not even a hint or notion that she was playing a game. "I don't want you to close your eyes. Ever. Not even at the end. Can you do that?"

He nodded slowly, understanding immediately. They were doing this together or not at all. "Yes," he said hoarsely. "I can do that."

It was awkward at first. As he had known it would be. Aria didn't know where to put her hands. Ethan wasn't sure he could do this with someone watching.

He kneeled in the vee of her thighs and draped her legs over his knees. Now she was open to him. His breathing was ragged, too loud perhaps in the quiet room.

When he placed his left hand on his thigh and took his shaft in his right hand, her gaze was riveted. "Does that feel good?" she asked, the words barely audible.

Nodding, he ran his thumb up and down the shaft slowly. He was so hard it was painful to touch himself. Having Aria stare so raptly only made it worse.

The inclination to close his eyes was almost over-powering. He hadn't realized that keeping his promise would be so difficult. "Touch your breasts," he said. "Let me see how good they feel."

She blinked in surprise, but she didn't challenge his command. Hesitantly, she cupped her modest curves in her palms and pushed them toward each other, plumping them into two lovely mounds.

Holy hell. Fire shot through his groin. He gasped and tugged his hand roughly over his sex.

Aria's voice penetrated the haze of arousal. "Ethan. Open your eyes."

Until her sharp-edged command, he hadn't even realized his failure. He nodded. "Sorry."

Holding her gaze was the most incredibly difficult thing he had ever had to do. And the most incendiary.

He was a man. He jerked off. That was life. But this was different. Every stroke of his own hand on his own flesh felt like Aria was touching him. Her gaze was almost tactile. When she licked her lips, he could feel her tongue on *his* lips. His climax writhed toward the surface like an angry, insatiable beast.

His hand moved faster.

He gasped for breath. The force of his movements rocked the bed.

Every time he tried, unknowingly, to close his eyes, her voice drew him back. Those blue irises held him captive, channeled some mystical feminine sorcery that increased the pleasure a thousandfold.

"Aria!" he groaned and shot his essence across her soft curves, coming and coming and coming until he thought there would be nothing left of him.

When it was over, he took a moment to clean them both and then he collapsed on top of her. The room was silent but for the wild beating of his heart in his ears.

Aria stroked his hair, murmuring his name over and over in comforting tones.

Good Lord. What had she done to him?

Aria slept fitfully in Ethan's arms for most of the night. He held her tightly, his face buried in her hair. It was so wonderful and sweet and unprecedented, it scared her to death.

Around five thirty or six in the morning, she slipped away and returned to her own room, where she tumbled into bed and slept for another hour. Even that was not enough to erase the extraordinary memory of what had happened between them.

When she awoke for good sometime after seven, every moment of last night played in her head like a Technicolor movie, complete with sound effects. Only this cinema was far more real, because it captured the eroticism of touch and the arousing scent of warm skin and an avalanche of heart-wrenching emotion that left her feeling raw and unsure of herself.

How was she ever going to face him today? How was she going to pretend that she didn't love him? Ethan being Ethan would put two and two together pretty quickly. Aria had been the instigator for the final portion of last night's festivities. Eventually, it would occur to him that she had been hoping to break through his emotional barriers and force him to admit he loved her.

And then he would be angry.

If that had been her motive, it hadn't been intentional. She didn't want a man who had to be tricked into loving her. For years she'd honestly believed she was over her pointless crush on Ethan. That he had moved on, and so had she. But on a cold, late-winter day in Royal— when he came back into her life so abruptly—it was as if all the lies she had ever told herself had dissolved in the joy of being with him again.

After dressing in a soft, slouchy sweatshirt and old jeans, she crept to the kitchen, desperate for a jolt of caffeine. Unfortunately, Ethan had beaten her to the coffeepot. He leaned against the counter, cup in hand, looking tired and rumpled, but incredibly sexy and appealing.

Her stomach flipped hard. "Hey," she said, searching desperately for a breezy tone. "Did you leave any for me?"

His gaze was impossible to read. No smile. Just a smoldering sexuality that made her shiver inwardly. "Help yourself," he said. "Cups are in the cabinet to the right of the sink." His dark hair stuck up in several places, perhaps because she had yanked at it during certain never-to-be-forgotten moments.

When she went up on tiptoe to grab an earthenware mug, she was aware of his gaze on her back. She tugged down her top self-consciously and poured herself a drink, adding sugar and milk generously.

Still Ethan didn't speak.

Though she risked burning her tongue, she took a few sips right off, unable to deal with this conversation without her coffee.

After three or four minutes, the silence was agonizing. She tried to smile, but it felt fake. "So what are you up to this morning? I assume you'll be at the club site all day?"

He refilled his cup. "Yes. I have back-to-back meetings from eleven till six. No rest for the weary."

Aria nodded. "I understand. I brought some dresses for the gala from home, but I thought I'd go out today and look for something new. Who can resist Houston stores? You know me. I love patronizing local businesses, but the fourth largest city in America? I'd be a fool not to at least window-shop. All the major designers are here. And I'm meeting friends for dinner, so don't worry about me. I may be late."

He came around the island, took the coffee cup from her hand and kissed her. The kiss was firm and heated, but not to the level of last night's excesses. Ethan's eyes crinkled at the corners afterward as his eyes warmed in a smile. "What's wrong, darlin'? Are you bashful this morning?"

She shrugged her shoulders. "Of course not. Why would I be?"

Ethan smoothed the hair from her face. "Can I ask you a personal question?"

She froze in his arms, sensing danger. "I suppose."

"How many men have you slept with? Before me?"

"That's not fair," she said. "I've never asked to compare notes about our love lives."

"Humor me." The teasing faded from his gaze. Now, if anything, he appeared troubled.

Aria thought about lying. He would never know. She could embellish her number enough to make herself seem like a typical twenty-eight-year-old woman. Unfortunately, she had never been adept at juggling the truth. "Two," she said baldly. "One during college and a second in Royal when you first moved to Houston." She really didn't know why he cared.

Her answer seemed to bother him. Well, that was too damn bad. "You want to share your number with me, Ethan?"

He scrubbed his face with both hands, wincing at her sarcasm. "I have to get ready for work."

"I know that."

"I'm sorry I won't be around to entertain you today."

Something about his demeanor flicked her on the raw. "I'm not a child who needs to be appeased with a lollipop. Go do whatever you have to do. I've got plenty to keep me occupied. In fact, you can forget I'm even here."

He folded his arms across his chest, his expression thunderous. "If I could do that, Aria, we wouldn't have a problem."

Thirteen

Aria wished desperately that she could simply fly back to Royal immediately and never have to see Ethan again. Cowardice and avoidance held a definite appeal. She was desperately glad the new renovation project was keeping him occupied.

It was better this way. Last night hadn't changed anything at all. He still didn't want to be tied to anyone, despite this false engagement. And if Aria allowed herself to weave silly daydreams about a future with Ethan, she was simply courting heartbreak.

On any given day, shopping at exclusive salons for a fabulous party dress would have been fun and exciting. As it was, Aria found her mind wandering time and again as she tried on one dress after another. Usually, she dressed to please herself. Now, after what had happened in Ethan's bed last night, it was impossible not to wonder what he would think when he saw her in satin and lace or even next to nothing at all.

She started at Neiman Marcus, which was the safe and obvious choice for a fancy outfit. Though the original flagship store was in Dallas, the Houston location at the Galleria was none too shabby. Aria spent a pleasant morning trying on dresses, but didn't find exactly what she was looking for. After lunch with a friend at a trendy downtown bistro in one of the high-rise hotels, she set out on foot to find a boutique she had heard about.

The River Seine was the brainchild of a Parisian transplant who had married an American and brought with her a distinctly French sensibility when it came to fashion. Though starting a business from scratch was challenging, the younger set in Houston had embraced Marie's designs with enthusiasm.

Aria picked out several casual outfits for spring and summer and then settled in to the serious business of selecting a gown for the gala, one that would turn heads. One stubborn male head in particular.

The theme for the fund-raising gala was "It's All in Black & White." Aria seldom wore black for formal occasions—she preferred a pop of color—but she found herself wanting to prove to Ethan that she was more sophisticated and worldly than he realized. Besides, white would look too virginal and sweet for what she had in mind.

She wanted to make him hungry. She wanted him to see her as a sexy, desirable woman.

One he couldn't live without.

Because the shop wasn't large, the inventory was, out of necessity, limited. Aria was beginning to give up on finding the perfect dress when the exuberant thirty-something Marie returned from the back one last time with an armful of black satin and tulle.

"Try this one," she said, beaming, her accent strong. "I forgot about it. A young lady took it home last week, and her parents wouldn't let her keep it to wear for prom, because it was, how you say it, too, um…"

Aria lifted an eyebrow. "Risqué?"

"Oui." Marie nodded. "The tags are still attached. If mademoiselle likes it, I give you nice discount, because it has been returned."

Aria took the dress into the tiny fitting room. As soon as she put it on, she understood exactly why a high-school girl had not been allowed to keep it. The dress was shockingly sensual.

The black satin gown, overlaid with intricate, tiny patterned black lace, was strapless. That part was not so unusual. Subtle boning kept the bodice in place. But the neckline plunged almost to the waist in front. And in the back…well, there was no back to speak of at all.

Aria managed to zip the frock and then stared at herself in the three-way mirror. Her breasts looked amazing, even without a bra. When she peered over her shoulder, she saw that the dress curved to fit her bottom as if had been sewn onto her. Below the knee, black tulle fluffed out, mermaid-style.

Marie had supplied a pair of black satin gloves that hugged Aria's arms and reached up past her elbows.

The designer/saleslady stood just outside the curtain. "Well," she said. "What do you think?"

Aria turned in a circle. Though she was completely clothed, she felt as if she was naked. The dress was designed to showcase a woman's body and to demand a man's attention. "What about jewelry?" she asked faintly.

Marie twitched the curtain. "May I look?"

"Yes, of course."

The Frenchwoman put her hands to her cheeks. "Ooh, la la. This is how I want my designs to look. You have the perfect body. Not too plump, not too skinny. A man will think of all those curves and not be able to sleep at night, *n'est-ce pas*?"

Her naughty amusement made Aria smile. "I've never worn anything so revealing."

The Frenchwoman shrugged, a Gallic gesture that indicated her disdain for such prudish concerns. "You are young and strong and attractive. Now is the time to enjoy your beauty. And besides, you show more of yourself at the beach, is not true?"

Aria had to admit the designer had a point. Besides, it was supposed to be in the eighties tomorrow. "And the jewelry?"

"An old-fashioned strand of jet beads to dangle in this lovely valley." She brushed the tops of Aria's breasts. "And matching earrings. But studs only. Not too much."

Aria trusted the other woman's intuition when it came to accessories, though she was not at all sure about wearing the outrageous gown.

Even so, she plunked down her American Express card and paid for all the glitz and glamour without a single qualm. Go big or go home. Wasn't that what people said?

She had the inescapable feeling that tonight and tomorrow night were her absolute last chances to win Ethan over to her way of thinking, to persuade him that he wasn't his father, and that he wasn't a man who would ever cheat on or hurt a woman he cared about.

In her gut, she knew she was heading for heartbreak, but she couldn't give up on him. Not yet.

With no shopping left to do, she had all of her packages dispatched to Ethan's condo. She would have preferred a quiet, intimate evening at Ethan's place if he had asked her to change her plans. But he had been oddly silent all day. No texts. No phone calls.

Because she wanted to give him his space, she went ahead with her original agenda and joined a trio of old college friends for the evening meal. The girls' night was fun—plenty of laughter and catching up—but it didn't fill the ache in her heart. She was already grieving the loss of Ethan. And it hadn't even happened yet.

It was almost ten when she returned to Ethan's condo.

The concierge was one she hadn't met yet. "Has Mr. Barringer returned this evening?" she asked.

"I haven't seen him, ma'am. But I only came on duty at eight."

Aria thanked him and crossed to the bank of elevators. Was Ethan upstairs? Her heart pounded.

It was a distinct letdown when she used her key, let herself in and found the apartment silent and deserted.

She found all of her packages neatly stacked just inside the door, so she carried them to her room.

After that, she spent an hour in the den watching HGTV. When she started yawning, she glanced at her watch and decided to call it a night. Disappointment curled in her stomach, but she ignored it staunchly. Ethan was a busy man. He wasn't her boyfriend. He was merely letting her stay with him so she wouldn't have to go to a hotel.

And he wasn't lying dead in a ditch, or surely some-one would have contacted her.

Grinning wryly at her own dark humor, she went to her room and got ready for bed. Tomorrow night was the gala. The next morning, she would fly back to Royal. Her life would go back to normal.

Why was that prospect so very dismal?

Ethan's day had been one hellish snafu after another. Around four o'clock, he actually thought his luck was improving. He'd had visions of calling Aria and offer-ing to take her out to dinner.

But just about then, he'd discovered that two of the hotel walls they had planned on ripping out were load-bearing. Which meant calling in the architect and doing a quick revamp of the existing site plan to see how much had to be scrapped and which of the original blueprints could be left intact.

It was like pulling a thread in a tapestry. One thing led to another and another and another.

In the end, the worst of the problem had been resolved over a very, very late dinner at a local steak-house, but the entire affair had left him exhausted.

When he made it to the condo and quietly let him-self in, it was after midnight. He had entertained the unlikely hope that Aria might have waited up for him.

He should have known better. He'd done a pretty damn good job of convincing her that he didn't need her.

After stopping by his suite to strip off his shirt and kick off his shoes and socks, he wandered barefoot down the hall. If Aria's door had been closed, he abso-lutely wouldn't have opened it. That would have been creepy.

But it was ajar. He put his hand on the edge and eased it the tiniest bit wider. She hadn't closed the drapes, and in the full moon he could see her silhouette against the white sheets. She had one arm flung over her head. Her hair tumbled across the pillow.

Again, that odd pain assaulted his chest. For the first time, he allowed himself to remember a moment years ago when he had wondered if they might make a go of it. Aria had been home from college on fall break, and the two of them had run into each other at a party.

She had been incandescent that night. Young. Full of life. He had just found out that his father was divorcing his *second* wife. The knowledge had burned in Ethan's gut like acid.

Aria had been so pleased to see him, and the two of them had talked for an hour in a small corner of their host's apartment. Ethan remembered the evening in vivid detail. Aria had worn ripped jeans and a fuzzy lavender cropped sweater that exposed her navel.

Ethan's bad mood had gradually dissipated. By the end of the night, he had actually felt lighthearted enough to walk Aria home and think about kissing her good-night.

They'd been laughing and teasing each other. Old friends. Very old friends. Comfortable with each other, yet still very aware of the sexual vibe between them, the tug of attraction that had existed since they grew old enough to understand what such things meant.

But at the final minute, he'd pulled himself back from the edge, because he hadn't been sure.

Even then, he had known Aria was disappointed in him.

Now here they were, years later. The memory of last night made him want to steal inside that partly open door and climb into bed with her.

He didn't even have to have sex, though God knew that would have been amazing. Tonight, though, he craved the thought of sleeping with her. Just sleeping.

The longer he stood there, the more his body ached. His sex hardened. His breathing quickened. He wanted her. Endlessly. Always. What was he going to do about it?

The next morning, he woke up early, ready to confront his beautiful houseguest and make plans for the big evening. His mood took a dive when he found a note on the kitchen table.

I'm headed down to the beach at Galveston with a friend. I'll be back in plenty of time to change for the gala. See you then. Hugs, Aria

The note was breezy and friendly, exactly like her. Of course she had friends. A million of them. And the fact that she hadn't mentioned whether or not the beach friend was male or female didn't bother Ethan at all.

Grumpy and frustrated, he headed for work. At least he had tonight to look forward to. And after the fund-raising gala was over, well, only time would tell.

His day was marginally better than the day before, but not much. There were no major crises, though when he found himself barking at his employees and having to apologize time and again, he realized that he was in a bad way. His head ached as if he had been up all night drinking, when in fact, he was stone-cold sober.

The fact that he had absolutely no idea what Aria was thinking drove him crazy. Was she glad to be ac-companying him to the gala tonight? Or was he sim-ply a chauffeur?

Ryder Currin had planned for a formal, sit-down din-ner at this event, and dancing afterward. The thought of other men touching Aria made Ethan's chest tighten. He felt possessive. Protective.

Aria would not react well to either of those reactions from him. She was independent, and she was not inter-ested in a one-way relationship. Any man who might one day marry her and give her babies would have to accept her as a full partner.

By the time Ethan's crew clocked out at four, jubi-lant at getting paid for an hour of heading home early, Ethan was more than ready to be done for the weekend.

He drove back to the condo in heavy traffic, drum-ming his hands on the steering wheel. It seemed like a week since he had seen and spoken with Aria, not merely a day and a half.

She was nowhere in sight when he got home, but he heard sounds from her bedroom, enough to reassure him that she had indeed made it back from Galveston. Damn straight. She was his date for the night.

He showered and changed into his tux, wrestling with the bow tie and trying to pretend his hands weren't clumsy with nerves.

Because he and Aria had both been asked by the TCC board to be on hand early at the gala, they were supposed to leave at five thirty. The hotel wasn't far. But they would be battling rush hour.

Ethan strode to the foyer, pulled his phone from his pocket and called downstairs to have the car brought up from the garage.

He glanced at his watch for the millionth time. "Aria," he bellowed. "We're gonna be late. Where are you?"

A small, quiet voice from the hallway behind him arrested his attention. "I'm right here, Ethan. You don't have to shout."

Ethan spun on his heel and sucked in his breath. "Aria?"

Fourteen

Aria managed a small smile. "You were expecting someone else?"

She was finding it a bit hard to breathe. As handsome as Ethan was in casual wear or work clothes or even a sport coat and tie, in formal evening attire he was magnificent. His shoulders were a million miles wide. His waist was trim, and his legs were long and masculine.

Maybe this was why the Victorians invented smelling salts.

She gripped her satin evening clutch. "I'm ready."

She could swear he paled when he saw her.

He frowned. "Don't you have a shawl or a coat or something?"

The question was confusing. "It's hot outside. And humid. I think I'll be fine."

His gaze lingered on her cleavage. "You look stunning."

The compliment was almost grudgingly bestowed.

"Thank you." Disappointment threatened to dampen her excitement for the evening. She had expected him to snatch her up and tell her she was beautiful and that he couldn't wait to kiss her and make love to her.

Instead, he was acting as if her dress was a personal affront.

He didn't even take her arm as they exited the condo and made their way to the elevator.

The concierge down in the lobby—on the other hand—had to pick his jaw off the floor when he saw her dress. Claude was an older gentlemen, seventy if he was a day. He shook his head with a twinkle in his eye. "That's one fine dress, Ms. Jensen. You look like a movie star. Mind if I snap a selfie with you? The wife will get a kick out of it. She'll read all about the TCC gala in the papers tomorrow."

"Of course not."

Ethan glowered through the entire episode.

In the car, she snapped at him. "What is the matter with you? Poor Claude thought he had done something wrong."

"I'll put an extra fifty in his pocket later tonight."

"That's not an answer."

"I don't like your dress."

The outright insult shocked her speechless for a moment. Then she recovered. "And I don't really care. In case you've forgotten, I'm only a *fake* fiancée, not a real one, so your opinion means nothing to me."

"Are you even wearing anything at all underneath that getup?"

When she shot him a sideways glance, she saw that his hands were white-knuckled on the steering wheel and his neck was bright red above the collar of his shirt. His jaw was granite.

"Don't worry," she said wryly, skirting the issue. "I won't embarrass you in front of your mom and John."

"They won't even be here," he said tersely. "They left this morning to visit a sick friend in San Francisco. They'll be back tomorrow night."

Aria gaped at him. "Then we don't have to pretend to be a couple." The news should have relieved her. And it did. Of course it did. Putting on a show before them had made her feel horribly guilty.

"Aren't you forgetting about Harmon Porter?"

"I don't even care about him anymore. He wouldn't confront me in such a public setting. We can drop the act."

"You seem awfully eager to break our engagement," he growled, jerking the wheel to avoid a car that had slammed on its brakes right in front of them.

The avoided collision shook Aria back to her senses. "I don't want to fight with you this evening, Ethan. It's an important night for the new club. We should keep our personal business out of this."

She had been so happy and excited, and now the day fell flat. Why could the two of them never seem to get things right?

Without warning, Ethan pulled into a dimly lit parking garage two blocks away from the hotel where the gala was being held. Surely he didn't expect them to walk from here. Her stiletto heels were almost four inches high.

He lowered the window, took a ticket and found several empty spots in a deserted section of the concrete tower. With the engine running and the A/C still pumping out cold air, he shoved the car into Park and turned to face her.

"I have to know something," he said.

She sniffed and stared out the windshield. "I'm not answering the underwear question."

"Funny. Very funny."

"Then what?"

"When we get home tonight, what do you think is going to happen between us?"

"How should I know? You disappear for hours at a time. First you want me. Then you don't. I've got emotional whiplash."

"I told you before that you'd have to initiate sex because I don't want there to be any hint that we're exchanging sex for your father's two-point-five mil."

"I remember. But for the record, I'm pretty sure that nothing I know how to do in the bedroom would be worth that amount anyway, so it's a moot point."

"That dress makes me crazy."

His brooding admission sounded accusatory at best.

"I didn't buy this dress for you. I bought it for me. And I think I look pretty damn good. So you can take your stupid opinion and go stuff it."

It was a great retort, a scathing comeback. Too bad it wasn't true. Of course she had bought the dress for

Ethan. Every woman in love wanted her man to think she looked beautiful and desirable. Aria was no different.

Apparently, she had badly miscalculated. Now, the only thing to do was try to save face.

Without warning, he unfastened his seat belt and leaned across the low console. "Do you have extra lipstick in that tiny purse?"

She cocked her head, wondering if he had gone round the bend. "Um, yes, but what—"

"Good." His mouth slammed down over hers, stealing every ounce of oxygen from her lungs. His kiss was raw. Desperate. Perhaps even lacking in technique.

Aria clung to his shoulders, moaning low in her throat. He tasted good. And he felt even better. She strained against him. "Ethan…"

"Shhh." He kissed her harder, his teeth bruising her lips. "We do better when we don't talk." His hand slid inside the bodice of her dress, palming her breast.

His droll comment amused her, but she couldn't catch her breath long enough to actually laugh. She unbuttoned two buttons on his shirt and touched hot male skin. "Do we have to go to this party? I can think of lots better ways to entertain ourselves tonight."

He shuddered and rested his forehead against hers, his chest heaving. "Don't say that. Even in jest. I want you right now."

"I've never had sex in a parking garage. Do you think it's against the law?" She put her hand on his taut thigh, her fingers dangerously close to the large bulge beneath his trousers. "You do have tinted windows in the back."

"Stop. I mean it. Stop." He pulled back, wild-eyed. "How long did it take you to get your hair up in that fancy knot thing?"

She grimaced. "Too long for you to mess it up."

"That's what I was afraid of." His grim disappointment was comical.

"You don't really hate my dress at all, do you?" she said.

His dark-eyed gaze seared her. "What do you think? The part I hate is knowing that every other man at that party tonight is going to be lusting after you."

"I think you're overstating the case. All the women will be dressed up. But I appreciate the compliment."

He ran his finger from her collarbone down the shadowy valley between her breasts, all the way to where the vee of her dress finally came to a halt. "You have no idea how truly magnificent you are. You never have."

Aria wrinkled her nose. "Let's talk about something else." His praise made her uneasy.

"Okay." He nodded slowly. "How about the way I want to strip you naked later. But wait. I can't. You have to ask me first."

She smothered a grin unsuccessfully. "I'm not sure you understand the rules of this passive beta-male approach. But then again, I don't have any complaints so far."

He cupped her face in his big, slightly rough palms. His eyes glittered with emotion. "I have never wanted any woman the way I want you right now."

Her stomach quivered. His sexuality was a living,

breathing force between them. She wanted to melt against him and never let go.

But even in the midst of madness, some latent sense of self-preservation reminded her that nothing had changed. Ethan Barringer was not a man who could be pinned down by any woman. He didn't believe in everlasting love. He didn't want her devotion or her heart.

"I want you, too, Ethan. Really I do. And if we didn't have responsibilities, I'd say to heck with this party. We'd climb in the back and act like crazy teenagers. But you're in charge of the entire renovation, and I'm the one who has to make sure the new club runs as smoothly as the TCC in Royal does, so our personal wishes can't be front and center tonight."

No matter how much she wanted to see him naked again.

He glanced at the digital clock on the dash and cursed. "You're right. Of course." The admission was made grudgingly. Stiffly. As if it had been dragged out of him.

Aria was no less disappointed, but she thought it best not to wear her heart on her sleeve. It wouldn't hurt for Ethan to wonder about her. She'd fallen into his arms and into his bed far too easily. Yet he hadn't wanted to keep her for his own. Maybe it was time to show him she wasn't some plaything he could pick up and put down when the mood struck him.

She straightened her dress while Ethan moved back into the driver's seat. He didn't say another word as he shot out of the garage and merged into the stream of traffic. At the hotel, they had to wait their turn to drop off the car with valet parking.

Already, despite the fact that Ethan and Aria were early, a stream of elegantly dressed men and women were making their way inside.

"So why is Ryder Currin hosting this gala tonight?" Aria asked. "I've been meaning to ask you that."

Ethan tapped the gas and inched forward, keeping his eye on the pedestrians. "My personal guess is that he's making a big splash to show he should be the first president of the new club."

"That's what I thought. I can't begin to imagine how much this is costing. The ice sculptures. The fresh flowers. Musicians. And that's not even talking about the food and the venue."

The gala was being held in one of the largest ballrooms at one of the premier hotels in the city. The guest list was a veritable who's who of Houston society, plus a sizable contingent of men and women from Royal. If Ryder Currin was hoping to score points in his battle with Sterling Perry, this event was a great way to start.

At last, the car was taken off their hands, and Ethan and Aria were able to head inside. Ethan took her elbow as they ascended the steps. His firm grip made her skin tingle.

Aria had been completely correct about the dress she bought. It was far from being the most outrageous frock present. The female guests' attire ran the gamut, from conventionally restrained to wildly flamboyant. Her gown's daring style fell somewhere in between.

As soon as they entered the ballroom, several people

demanded Ethan's attention. He shot her an apologetic look as he dove into one conversation after another. She smiled wryly, not at all surprised. Ethan would be president of the TCC one day in the future, she had no doubt.

His charisma and charm, combined with a reputation for trustworthiness, made him a logical choice. Even as young as he was, many people deferred to his opinions and wanted to do business with him.

After making a few strategic contacts of her own, she scanned the room, trying to mentally name as many of the guests as she could. As she began setting up membership files for the new club, it would be extremely helpful if she already knew names and faces.

The key players were in attendance, of course. Sterling Perry was holding court in the center of a semicircle of younger men who appeared to be hanging on his every word. Now that Ryder Currin had staged his splashy event, surely Sterling would have to come up with something similar if he wanted to stay in the race for president.

Just as Aria was wishing Ethan wasn't quite so far away on the other side of the room, a familiar voice called her name.

"Aria! You look fabulous."

Aria turned and saw Abby and Brad Price bearing down on her, both of them smiling widely. She hugged them both. "I'm so glad you're here," she said. "It's been ages since I've seen you." A decade older than Aria and Ethan, Abby Langley Price was both gorgeous *and* a power broker in her own right. She had been one of the first women admitted into the Texas Cattleman's Club in Royal, and had mentored Aria over the years, particularly when it came to this new venture in Houston.

The tall, striking redhead waved a slender arm. "Isn't this amazing? Ryder has outdone himself."

Her husband rolled his eyes. "Come on, darlin'. You know this is a game. Sterling will have his day in the sun."

Abby sniffed. "Sterling Perry is all flash and thousand-dollar shoes. I can't imagine why you defend the man."

Aria chuckled. "Have I walked into the middle of a marital fight?"

Brad shook his head. "Not at all. We're just like everyone else, wondering who will end up being president. I know there's bad blood between the two men from a long time ago, but I don't know why. No one really talks about it."

"They have been recently," Aria said. "I kept hearing snippets of gossip at the ground-breaking. Do you think it's all an attempt to stir up trouble?"

Abby nodded. "Makes sense. Sometimes you have to ruffle a few feathers to get what you want."

Her husband kissed her temple, his smile indulgent. "And that's why you're dangerous, my love." He grinned at Aria. "I see a buddy of mine I need to talk to. Try to keep my hotheaded wife out of trouble while I'm gone."

Angela Perry smoothed the skirt of her ice-blue gown and frowned when she realized her palms were damp. This was ridiculous. Just because Ryder Currin was in the room.

She'd been eyeing him unobtrusively for half an

hour now. The rags-to-riches oil baron was the center of attention tonight, a charming host with an appealing smile and a contagious laugh. Twice married with three grown children, Ryder was the kind of sexy that would never fade with age.

And he had mentioned having dinner with *her*.

Life was short. Angela had learned not to wait for things to come to her. Instead, she went after what she wanted.

Tonight, that was Ryder.

She cooled her heels until there was a lull in the crowd at his side. Then she pinned on a confident smile and approached him. "Ryder. Wonderful party. You've outdone yourself."

When he turned and his eyes flashed navy with heat, that hot gaze raked her from head to toe and made her feel naked. But just as quickly as it had kindled, the lustful look was gone.

His smile was conventional. "Angela. You're lovelier than ever tonight."

"Thank you."

She felt gauche suddenly. And unsure of herself. Had she imagined the jolt of attraction between them? He had done it to her again. Made her doubt. Made her wonder.

"Your father seems to be enjoying himself," he said.

Ryder's laconic sarcasm drew a smile from her in spite of her discomfort. "He hates that you thought of this fund-raising gala idea before he did, but of course, he had to be here. Who knows how he'll retaliate."

"Oh, well," Ryder said, "it's all for the good of the new club."

"Ryder…" Her heart was lodged in her throat, making it hard to breathe.

He shot her a sideways look, tinged with impatience. Or was it something else? "Yes?"

"You mentioned having dinner with me."

For a moment, she knew she had gotten through to him. He looked flummoxed at first, then uncomfortable, and lastly—most definitely—interested. "It's a very busy time," he said, his gaze scanning the room as if he was looking for someone.

She put a hand on his arm. "I was glad you asked me. It sounded like fun. I'm free next Friday. What do you say?"

When she touched his arm she felt him stiffen. His entire body seemed to freeze.

And then he took a step backward, causing her hand to fall away.

Her stomach knotted.

Ryder's jaw tightened. He didn't quite meet her eyes. "I don't think that's a good idea, Angela. Sterling wouldn't like it, and I won't tiptoe behind his back."

She should have walked away and preserved what was left of her pride. But her disappointment was such that she had to push back. "I don't understand," she said quietly. "It was your idea. Remember?"

The muscles in his throat worked. His hands fisted at his sides. "I may have mentioned it," he said. "But if I did, it was one of those things people toss out in conversation. A social nicety."

Her temper sparked. "You're saying you *accidentally* mentioned having dinner with me? Good Lord, Ryder. I know you're fifty but I didn't think senility had set in." She lowered her voice. "I could have sworn you were attracted to me. Was I wrong?"

He turned to face her, his hands jammed in his pockets. His gaze seared her. "Drop it, Angela. We both know it's a terrible idea. We're the Hatfields and the McCoys. Romeo and Juliet. You get the picture."

Ice filled the space where her heart had beaten a moment ago. "No," she said carefully, trying not to let him see how much he had hurt her. "We're not feuding enemies. And we're not doomed lovers. Apparently we're nothing at all. Excuse me, Mr. Currin. I have other guests to see. Friends. Neighbors. People who aren't spineless bastards."

Fifteen

Ryder cursed viciously beneath his breath as he watched Angela Perry walk away. Her body was poetry in motion. Any man would appreciate her feminine sexuality, not just Ryder.

He had handled that very badly.

She was right, of course. He *was* attracted to her. But the spontaneous dinner invitation at the groundbreaking ceremony had been a very bad idea. Sterling would have a coronary if he knew Ryder was dating one of his daughters.

Even worse, Sterling would assume Ryder was with Angela as part of some Machiavellian plot to sabotage Sterling's plans to head up the new club. Nothing could be further from the truth.

Yes, Ryder did want to be president. And yes, he was

interested in Angela. But those two realities had nothing in common.

Besides, if he and Angela ever dated even casually, someone might dig up dirt from the past and use it to hurt Angela. Ryder couldn't have that on his conscience. It was one thing for Sterling and Ryder to hold a decades-long grudge. Ryder wouldn't allow Angela to be caught in the middle.

When he saw Ethan Barringer approaching, he forced himself to concentrate on the central purpose of the evening. His personal life had long taken a back seat to business. Tonight would be no different.

Even so, his gaze followed Angela for several moments until she ended up on the far side of the enormous ballroom.

Ethan approached and shook his hand. "Great party, Mr. Currin."

"Call me Ryder, please. Did your boss send you over here to spy on me and dig up information?"

Ethan grinned. "No, sir. I pretty much stick to my renovation project. Sterling goes his own way in other areas."

"Ah, you're a diplomat."

Barringer lifted a shoulder. "Let's just say I never burn bridges if I can help it."

"I saw you come in with Aria Jensen. I was glad to hear she's coordinating the setup for all our new systems at the Houston club. Everyone tells me she's top-notch."

"I've known her since we were kids. She's honest to a fault and as smart as they come."

"Do you think we can persuade her to move here to Houston?"

Barringer seemed shocked. "Here?"

Ryder cocked his head, wondering if he had misread the signals. "Aren't the two of you an item? I assumed she might be wanting to relocate. I could put in an official request."

The younger man's face was suddenly hard to read. But he didn't seem happy about the conversation. Quite the opposite. "I don't think Aria has any interest at all in leaving Royal."

"Ah. But don't *you* live here in Houston?"

"Yes."

Ryder hadn't gotten where he was today by being thick-headed. But he pressed on. "Women are not the easiest creatures on the planet. I should know. I have two daughters, and I've had more than one wife, so I speak from experience. Don't let her get away."

Barringer's cheeks flushed. "No offense, sir, but I'm not really the marrying kind."

"Oh." Now Ryder was intrigued. "That sounds like a line from an old cowboy movie. Care to elaborate?"

"I don't actually."

The terse retort almost elicited a laugh from Ryder, but he sensed the younger man wouldn't share his amusement, so he kept his face straight and changed the subject. A short time later, several more people joined them. The conversation broadened, and Ryder watched with some regret as Ethan Barringer walked away.

Sterling Perry's CEO had a reputation for straight-shooting, something the namesake of Perry Holdings did not. Ryder wondered if the two men ever butted heads over ethical questions. Nevertheless, it pleased Ryder to know that Ethan was in charge of the hotel renovation for the Houston club. Everything would be done right.

Soon, a new group of guests demanded his attention. He sighed inwardly and forced himself to engage in pleasantries. He could no longer see Angela. She was lost in the crowd.

Angela Perry was so embarrassed and humiliated she wanted to crawl in a hole and die. Instead, she had to smile and mingle and pretend she was actually enjoying this stupid party.

What had possessed her to confront Ryder in such a public venue? Was that why he had been such an ass? Or was his rejection exactly what it seemed?

Her cheeks still burned.

It astonished her to realize she was near tears. Since when did a man's opinion rattle her to such an extent?

Unfortunately, Tatiana was nearby. Angela didn't want her friend to know what had happened, not after Tatiana had specifically warned her about Ryder just a few days ago at the ground-breaking.

To avoid any unpleasant confrontations or questions, Angela ducked into the closest ladies' room and locked herself in an opulent stall. With the commode lid down and plenty of tissue to mop up her tears, she let the sadness wash over her.

The bathroom consisted of an outer foyer with comfortable armchairs and lighted mirrors and an inner chamber with marble sinks and individual facilities behind tall wooden doors.

No one would notice if Angela stayed in here all night. Only her family, perhaps, might take note of her absence.

Eventually, the tears ran out. After that, she felt a bit foolish. Ryder was just a man. She had a little crush. No biggie. She would get over it. Probably. And it wasn't like she had to see him every day.

With the help of a disposable wipe from her purse and the small stash of miniature-sized makeup supplies she carried with her, she managed to erase the evidence of her sob-fest. Or at least the worst of it. It wouldn't do for Ryder Currin to think he had wounded her. The man was far too arrogant as it was. She couldn't believe she had let him get to her so easily.

Just as she was preparing to exit the stall and return to the party, she heard the outer door open and close. Two people came in, or even three. They were speaking in low murmurs, almost as if they were being intentionally secretive.

Now she really felt trapped. She didn't want to burst out in the middle of a confidential conversation. Good grief.

She sat back down on the commode lid.

One of the voices seemed to come closer…maybe near the sinks?

Water turned on, then off.

The hushed whisper sounded sinister. "I can't believe he has the gall to even speak to Angela after what he did with her mother."

"What kind of sick monster has an affair with one woman and then when the mother is long dead tries to sleep with her daughter?"

Angela's world went dark for a split second and then the heat of rage shot everything back into sharp focus. Stricken, dumbfounded, she strained to listen. The two voices were so muffled it was difficult to make out the words.

"I heard that Ryder blackmailed Angela's mother. Swore to her he would tell Sterling about the affair unless she made her father leave Ryder a parcel of land in his will."

"Because Ryder was nothing but a ranch hand, right?"

"And Sterling was being forced by his father-in-law to work as foreman on the ranch and learn the business from the ground up."

"Old Sterling thought he was going to inherit it all, but Ryder was bequeathed that one piece of land outside of Houston that just happened to have oil."

"Which is how he got to be richer than Midas."

"Do you think he's already slept with Angela? What's his game?"

"Well, maybe she reminds him of her mother. Maybe he really loved the mom. Tamara. Wasn't that her name?"

"Poor Angela."

"Yeah…"

"I wish she…"

The doors opened and shut again, and the voices faded away.

Angela was frozen in place. Her brain functioned enough to tell her she was in shock, but she couldn't move.

Ryder must be planning to *use* her for some inexplicable reason. How had she ever thought he was truly interested in *her*? And why had she let herself get caught up in the pull of attraction that was apparently nothing but an act? The pain in her chest made it hard to breathe.

At last, after an undetermined amount of time had passed, she stood up and unlocked the door. Just as she exited the stall, a gaggle of college-aged girls burst into the outer portion of the bathroom, laughing and talking. Their fresh-faced enthusiasm was painful to witness.

Her whole world had been obliterated in an instant.

Aria watched Ethan work the room, feeling a combination of pride and impatience. She wanted to be alone with him. Even during the elaborate sit-down dinner, she'd been forced to share him with their fellow diners.

Both of them were doing their very best for the newly birthed TCC tonight. No one could fault them. They hadn't even slipped away to a deserted hotel room like they had at the ground-breaking.

That particular memory made her shiver. In a good way.

Ethan stood out in a roomful of handsome alpha males. He carried himself with confidence and assurance, and yet he was endlessly approachable. Whether it was a silver-haired octogenarian matriarch or a newly minted millionaire on the Houston social scene who was dying to be admitted to the club, Ethan handled the interactions with wit and charm.

Talking to Abby Price tonight had been a watershed moment for Aria, reminding her of how important it was not to back down from difficult challenges. Her friend had never been afraid to ask for what she wanted, or even to demand it, if the situation arose.

Maybe Aria had been handling this situation with Ethan all wrong. What would happen if she confessed she was in love with him? If she pointed out how good they were together? Sure, she risked his rejection, but at the rate they were going now, she was going to end things with him soon, anyway.

The thought of gambling her entire future on one roll of the dice later tonight made her stomach clench with nausea. She had always played by the rules. Could she change the habits of a lifetime?

If she tried this, and it failed, not only would she lose Ethan as her potential "forever" lover and life partner, but she could also lose her best friend.

The thought of that crushed her.

These past few weeks after he reappeared in her life had been so incredibly wonderful. Would it be better to take what little he had to give and simply be grateful? Or were scraps of affection worse than nothing at all?

The final two hours of the gala seemed to drag on forever.

She was trying to hide a yawn behind her hand when a familiar voice spoke at her ear. "May I have this dance?"

Her heart stumbled. "Ethan? Where did you come from? I didn't see you."

His smile was quizzical. "You were a million miles away. And your expression seemed awfully serious for a party. Everything okay?"

She nodded slowly, looking up into his dark brown eyes. Tonight those beautiful irises seemed to sparkle with glints of amber. Or maybe that was the chandeliers casting a reflection.

"I'm fine," she said. "Better than fine."

"You want to dance?"

"Are you kidding? I've waited all night for this."

He pulled her close and settled one large, warm palm on her bare back. Though she couldn't think of a single time in the past when they had danced together, now they moved as one, drifting across the dance floor in perfect harmony.

Ethan steered her between the other couples effortlessly. He held her tightly, and she pressed her cheek to his shoulder. They danced heart-to-heart, not speaking. The music washed over them—timeless, romantic tunes made for a man and a woman to connect on the dance floor.

One song segued into the next. Aria inhaled Ethan's familiar scent, a combination of lime-based cologne and starched cotton. His body was warm and hard against hers. Though she was entirely capable of taking care of herself, in Ethan's arms, she felt cherished and protected. Safe. Loved.

In the midst of all of her soul-searching, there was a third alternative she hadn't considered. One that was painful in its own way. Maybe Ethan *did* love her, but not in the way she needed to be loved. It was possible he felt deep affection for her, and that same affection—combined with their mutual combustible attraction—

was fooling Aria into believing she might have a future with him.

Her heart shied away from that explanation.

She wanted Ethan to be head over heels in love with her. She needed to hear those rare and wonderful words. *I love you, Aria.* The lust they shared was all well and good, but passion needed a deep foundation if it was going to last for the long haul.

So she had a choice tonight. She could bury her head in the sand and enjoy the physical bliss while it lasted, or she could push for something more and risk losing everything.

Ethan's fingertips lightly traced her spine. The simple caress raised gooseflesh all over her body, though the ballroom was plenty warm. His body was so close to hers she could feel his heavy erection pressing against her belly. The feel of him, insistent and masculine, made her breathless with longing and the urgent craving to feel him inside her.

His voice rumbled in her ear, low and rough with desire. "I'm taking you home soon. I've had about all of this I can take. I want you naked in my bed. Any objections?"

She tipped back her head and smiled up at him. "I thought *I* had to be the one doing the asking."

His disgruntled scowl was comical. "To hell with that. I've been forced to look at you in this damned dress for hours. I deserve a medal for not taking you up against the wall already."

Suddenly, her mouth was dry and her sex throbbed

with an aching emptiness that was more than physical. She wanted Ethan in every way there was to have a man. She reached up and ruffled his hair. "I adore you, Ethan Barringer. The band's taking a break. Let's get something to drink. And then maybe we can slip out while no one is watching."

"I like the way you think, woman." His tight grin was feral, his expression possessive.

They made their way to the bar, but settled on ginger ales instead of anything more potent. Ethan was driving, and Aria wanted a clear head for what was to come.

Just as they were preparing to make their getaway, they spotted Ryder Currin, not twenty yards away. Aria wrinkled her nose. "Oh, shoot. I suppose we have to say our goodbyes. I don't want to be rude."

They took a few steps in Ryder's direction, and then Ethan grabbed Aria's arm. "Hold up a minute."

As they watched, Angela Perry walked up to Ryder and—if looks could be trusted from a distance— accosted him with an agitated diatribe. Ryder seemed first shocked, then angry in return.

He opened his mouth to speak, but never got a chance. Angela reared back and slapped him across the face with all the force of her open palm.

Then she turned on her heel and left.

Ethan and Aria backed up and tiptoed away carefully. Ethan lowered his voice. "I think we can skip the goodbyes. I don't think he'll even notice we're gone."

"What do you suppose that was about?"

"I have no idea."

* * *

I'm quivering with excitement. The taste of revenge is sweeter than I could ever have imagined, and tonight has certainly lived up to my expectations. I didn't even have to do very much except sit back and watch my plans unfold. Once I disseminated bits and pieces of the old gossip about Ryder Currin and Tamara Perry a few days ago, other people began to do my work for me.

How delicious. How perfectly justified. Watching Angela Perry slap Ryder Currin was more exhilarating than a shot of hundred-year-old Scotch. They all deserve to feel the pain I've felt...and to know what it's like to lose everything. An eye for an eye. I won't stop until Sterling Perry and Ryder Currin and their families are humiliated and broken and ruined beyond repair.

I will have my day in the sun. But even that won't ever undo the damage they have done to me and mine...

Sixteen

Ethan could barely concentrate on his driving. Having Aria two feet away in the close confines of the car, inhaling her delicate perfume, seeing her bare feet when she kicked off her high heels with a low groan, turned him inside out. He was in danger of losing control tonight.

He couldn't. He wouldn't.

Maybe.

He cleared his throat, searching desperately for some innocuous topic to take his mind off the fact that she wasn't wearing a bra beneath that drop-dead-sexy dress. "Harmon Porter was there tonight, but he never said a word to either of us. You know him better than I do. What do you think that means?"

Aria yawned and leaned back against the headrest.

"Maybe he's one of those men who get off on making idle threats. Maybe he's nothing but bluster. He has a reputation to uphold."

Ethan frowned, and the vehicle rolled to a stop at the red light. "Perhaps. But I don't think he'll take your defection so easily."

"Another woman will come along."

He reached across the console and put a hand on her thigh. "There's only one you."

Aria curled her fingers around his. "What a sweet thing to say."

His sex flexed and grew, causing him physical pain. If holding her hand did this to him, he was in too deep. "Make no mistake, darlin'. I'm not sweet. In fact, I'm gonna gobble you up first chance I get."

She propped one slender ankle on the dashboard, causing her frothy skirt to fall back, revealing a toned, shapely calf. "I'm *so* afraid."

His hand clenched her thigh. When the light turned green, he had to force himself to release her so he could hold the wheel. "Laugh all you want," he said gruffly, "but you're mine tonight."

Everything about this evening had left him on edge. Aria's incandescent sexuality in that damn dress. Ryder Currin's inexplicably bothersome remarks. Dancing with Aria for hours, when the band played on and on and everything seemed possible.

Ethan knew himself. He knew his strengths and his weaknesses. He had become wealthy as a young man by focusing on his work and taking calculated risks in business. That same philosophy didn't extend into his personal life, because it didn't work.

He wouldn't change who he was. Because to do so meant the possibility of hurting the very people he had sworn to protect.

When they made it home, surprisingly in one piece given his fractured mental state, Aria didn't even bother putting on her shoes. No one was in the lobby to see them except a sleepy-eyed Claude.

The old man perked up when Aria smiled at him. Ethan slipped the guy a folded hundred. "Thanks for all you do."

"No worries, Mr. Barringer. It's been quiet tonight."

Aria kissed the old man's cheek. "I took a bunch of pictures on my phone. I'll text them to you tomorrow, so your wife can see all the decorations."

Claude beamed. "That's mighty kind of you."

She grinned. "I would do it now, but this marble floor is cold on my feet. Good night, Claude."

Ethan hurried her into the elevator before she could change her mind. Without her shoes, she looked tiny beside him. The juxtaposition of the black dress against her creamy white skin was a stunning contrast. She still wore her above-the-elbow gloves.

When she began to take them off, he intervened. "Not yet," he said huskily. "I have plans for those."

Her eyes widened and a pale pink flush bloomed on her cheeks. "I see."

For half a second he pondered pressing the button that would halt the elevator. But the damn thing had a security camera. Even if he tossed something over the lens, there were other residents in the building. That particular fantasy would have to stay in the realm of his imagination.

On the top floor, the bell dinged quietly, and the doors whooshed open. Ethan managed to fumble only slightly with the key.

Aria stood beside him, not saying a word.

In the foyer, he kicked off his shoes and tossed his keys on the table. Aria dropped her shoes beside his.

He rotated his shoulders, suddenly feeling the fatigue of being "on" the entire evening. It hadn't been a relaxed social occasion for Aria and him. They had been working...mostly.

"Do you want a snack?" he asked. "Something to drink?"

She curled her arms around his waist and rested her cheek over his heart. "No. I'm good."

He pulled a few pins loose and stroked her hair, battling a tsunami of conflicting emotions. "I wish you didn't have to go home tomorrow."

She went still. "Actually," she said, her voice small and quiet, "I've decided to stay over one more day. I have a couple of committee meetings with one of the charities I support, so I made a reservation at the Hilton for tomorrow night. I didn't want to be in your way."

One more night. A reprieve. "Don't be silly," he said lightly. "You know I want you here. We'll go out for a nice dinner after work. Just the two of us. How does that sound?"

Aria unfastened his bow tie and left the ends undone. "Sounds like fun. And now?"

He scooped her up in his arms and carried her down the hall. "Now the Big Bad Wolf is going to have his way with you."

Aria clung to Ethan's strong neck, feeling giddy and excited and hopeful. She wasn't a tiny woman, but he carried her as if she weighed no more than a bag of feathers. Though he had shaved before the gala, already his sculpted jaw showed evidence of a dark shadow.

In his suite, she expected him to deposit her on the bed right away. But he took her by surprise, setting her gently on her feet. "First things first," he said hoarsely.

She honestly had no idea what he meant until he fetched a small chair and placed it in front of her. Then he sat at her knees.

"Ummm, Ethan?"

A shiver worked its way down her bare spine. Beneath the stiffened bodice of her gown, her nipples tightened painfully.

He took her hips in his hands, leaned back in the chair and smiled. "We have all night. I don't plan to waste a minute of it."

"Some people sleep during the night," she pointed out. In case he had forgotten.

Ethan shrugged. "Sleep is overrated."

"What are you going to do to me?" She couldn't help the quiver of anticipation in the blurted question.

He heard her arousal. And clearly, he liked it.

"Don't worry, Aria. You're in good hands."

She fidgeted, her bare toes curling into the thick pile of his bedroom carpet. "I've been on my feet all evening." She threw in a pout for good measure. "I'd really like to lie down."

Ethan's amused grin told her he saw through her attempt to take control of the moment. "Sorry, but we're just getting started. The bed can wait until later."

"I thought you wanted to have sex."

Heat flared in his gaze. His cheekbones flushed as his chest heaved with one sharp inhalation. "Patience, Aria. Patience."

It almost seemed as if he was giving himself that advice, as well. His hands shook visibly as he spanned her waist. He leaned forward, resting his forehead just below her breasts.

She had to touch him. It was impossible not to. Lightly, tentatively, she stroked the curves of his ears with her thumbs. The satin of her gloves made the gesture sensual, erotic.

"I love your hair," she whispered, running her fingers through the thick strands.

Ethan shuddered. He bent and slid his hands beneath the frothy skirt of her gown, finding her bare legs. Carefully, he stroked from her heels to her ankles to the backs of her knees. Erogenous zones she'd never discovered flared into life, turning her into a raging cauldron of hormones.

She expected him to move north, but all he did was play with the sensitive bend of her legs. It was the most diabolical thing she could have imagined. Her fingers clenched in his hair so hard he protested. "Easy, my sweet. Don't make me bald before my time."

Inside her head she was begging him. *Do something,*

for heaven's sake. Get on with it. But Ethan was not to be rushed.

At last, he released her skirt and sat back, breathing heavily. He shrugged out of his tux jacket, tossed it aside and rolled up his sleeves. His bow tie still dangled.

"Now?" she asked hopefully.

"Now, what?"

"The bed?"

He cocked his head, resting his hands, palms flat, on his hard thighs. His legs were splayed, drawing attention to the large bulge where the seams of his trousers met. "Have you always been so impatient?"

The mocking taunt was laden with sexual challenge. Her sex clenched. Moisture dewed her folds, even as her body ached for his possession. "What do you want from me?" she whispered. She would do anything to move things along…to get them from point A to point B. Over his shoulder she could see the pristine bed just waiting for them.

Ethan's gaze narrowed. "Put your hands behind your neck."

She blinked at him, trying to decipher the command, looking for hidden meanings. It was difficult to link her fingers, because the fabric of her gloves was so slippery.

The new posture thrust her breasts up and out, nearly spilling them from the lace-covered bodice. Ethan stood and traced the deep valley where the dress dipped in front, his touch marking her like a brand. "You like making men drool, don't you?"

She shook her head defiantly. "Not *men*. Only you." She maintained the position he had requested. Now

Ethan moved a step closer. He reached behind her head and manacled her wrists with one big hand. Then he kissed her roughly, letting her feel the scrape of his teeth, the rough pull of his kiss as he suckled her bottom lip.

Whimpering, she leaned into him, wanting desperately to be naked, wanting him to be naked, too. Ethan drew the kiss out endlessly, making love to her mouth, tormenting both of them.

When she thought she absolutely couldn't bear it any longer, he sat down again.

This time, he slid his arms around her waist.

She felt him reach for the tab of her zipper and slowly begin to lower it. There wasn't much real estate to cover. The zipper started almost at the base of her spine and was only about six inches long.

When she felt the fabric begin to give, she clutched the bodice to her chest, oddly shy.

Ethan's hands settled on the curves of her bottom. He murmured something beneath his breath, something she didn't quite catch. Aria closed her eyes, almost mad with wanting him.

Gently, inexorably, he began to drag the dress from her grasp. Gravity was a powerful force. Moments later, the gown pooled at her feet.

He nudged her legs. She stepped free of the luxuriant fabric.

When nothing happened after that, she opened her eyes.

Ethan had slumped back in the chair, looking as

if he'd been poleaxed. "My God," he said reverently. "You're incredible."

"Don't, Ethan." The words made her uncomfortable. She was glad he found her sexy but she wanted so much more than that.

Her protest made him frown. "Shall I tell you what I see?" He didn't wait for an answer. "I see hair as soft and golden as sunshine on an early summer morning. Tiny black studs that make me want to nibble your ears. A graceful neck and a delicate strand of jet beads that drape between two perfect breasts. A body that's both soft and strong and beckons a man to feast until he can't indulge anymore. And you wearing those damned sexy gloves and tiny undies that are probably against the law in several states… Hell, Aria, you could be a centerfold."

"I don't want to be a centerfold."

"What *do* you want?"

She sucked in a startled breath. There would never be a more perfect opening than that. But fear kept her quiet. "I want you," she said. "Just you."

Without waiting for him to respond, she leaned down and unbuttoned his shirt. Ethan was breathing heavily, his gaze barely focused. Perhaps the fact that her breasts were in his face might have had something to do with that.

When she dragged his shirt from his pants, he lurched to his feet. "Come on," he said, the words slurred, as if he had been drinking. "Don't take off a single other thing. I want to make love to you just like this."

They walked to the bed hand in hand. He lifted Aria

without ceremony and tumbled her onto the mattress. Then he removed the rest of his clothing and joined her. They lay facing each other, side by side.

She had seen the man naked more than once now. But his body never failed to take her breath away. It was a man's body. Broad-shouldered, muscular, powerfully sexual. His shaft thrust upward against his flat abdomen proudly. Aria curled her fingers around him.

Ethan stared.

Even Aria had to admit that the sight of her glove-clad hand against his sex was erotic. She used her thumb on the underside of his erection to stroke him. Slowly, she was beginning to learn what he liked. She no longer felt quite as tentative, nor as naive.

Ethan muttered something indecipherable and rolled to his back. As Aria leaned over him, her necklace shifted, draping around one breast, the glass beads cold against her heated skin. In that moment, she felt sensual, sexual. As if she had the power to bring him to his knees.

Though the prospect held a certain appeal, what she wanted was for him to admit he couldn't live without her.

Their gazes locked, his glazed with hunger, hers guarding a secret longing.

Ethan cupped the back of her neck with one big hand, pulling her down for a kiss. "The first time I saw you tonight," he muttered, "wearing those gloves, I nearly swallowed my tongue. You're exquisite, Aria. Every man's fantasy. I want to make love to you a million different ways, but my patience is eroding. If I don't get inside you soon, I might actually die."

His rueful smile tugged at her heart. He was so damn adorable and sexy.

She squeezed his shaft gently. "Who knew you had a glove fetish?"

He closed his eyes, groaning. "I didn't know," he muttered. "But now it's all I can think about."

"I'm here. In your bed. How do you want me tonight, sir?"

He lifted one eyelid, visibly intrigued. "You're offering me carte blanche? That's brave of you."

Her sex tightened at the implied threat. "I trust you, Ethan. I always have."

Without warning, he sat up and rolled off the bed. "Don't move."

In moments, he was back, carrying a handful of neckties.

Her mouth went dry. "What are those for?"

His wicked grin set off tiny explosions of arousal deep in her pelvis. "I think you know. Move up in the bed. And stretch your arms over your head. It's time to see whether you mean what you say."

The most incredible mixture of emotions washed through her body. Excitement. Uncertainty. Resolve.

Ethan wasted no time in executing his plan. His bed was a massive mahogany affair that had low pillars at each corner, sturdy enough for a man to use as hitching posts.

With an economy of motion Aria had to admire, despite her position, Ethan took her left wrist, knotted one of his ties around it, and then secured the other end to the bed. He repeated the process with her right hand. In less than three minutes, she was bound and at his mercy.

When she saw him glance back at her ankles, she shivered. "No. Please."

His expression softened. "Fair enough. But only because I want you more mobile than that when I take you." He stared at her, his gaze hot and getting hotter by the second.

Aria tried to swallow. She felt incredibly vulnerable. Did he understand what she was offering him? Did he understand how special this was for her? She was giving him everything.

Ethan sprawled beside her and traced a circle around one puckered nipple. "I can't decide where to start."

"Well, pick a place," she said.

Seventeen

Ethan grinned. The snap in her voice told him she was as turned on as he was and eager for the finale.

Still, he had to linger a moment more to enjoy the picture she made, sprawled with abandon in his bed. He moved between her legs and took one ankle in each hand. "Don't try to hide from me, Aria. You said this was my fantasy. I expect full compliance."

Her eyes widened. Her cheeks had been flushed before. Now the tide of rosy red spread down her throat and to her collarbone. Her chest heaved. "What am I supposed to do all tied up?"

"I'll make it easy," he said. "Close your eyes. I'll do all the work."

Her hands flexed against their bindings and she closed her eyes.

His sex swelled. Playtime was over. He simply didn't have it in him to wait any longer.

But first, he would pleasure her.

Starting at the delicate arches of her feet, he pressed kisses against her warm, scented skin, moving up along her legs and thighs and finally into the valley where she wept for him. With a few well-placed flicks of his tongue, she cried out and climaxed, whispering his name.

He left her only a moment, grabbed the protection he needed, rolled it on and reclaimed his position.

"I'm going to take you now. Hard and fast and long. Tell me you want me. But keep your eyes closed."

She arched her back, bit her lip and nodded. "I want you," she said faintly. "Please. Now."

He went forward onto his elbows and probed her soft, wet sex, filling her inch by inch. The fit was tight, the sensation akin to fiery bliss. When he thought she had taken all of him she could, she canted her hips and took him deeper.

He cried out her name, desperately trying to hold back the wall of rushing pleasure that threatened to drown him, to sweep him away to a place he'd never been willing to go.

Aria's body gripped him, drained him, made him weak. He was sorry now that her hands were tied. He wanted to feel her fingers in his hair when he came. But it was too late now. He was teetering on the edge.

His vision went black. *Aria. Aria.* He pounded into her. Mindless. Wild with hunger and need and something more.

And then the thread snapped. He came violently, endlessly. Slumping on top of her, he felt the hot sting of tears in his eyes.

Something had happened to him. Despite the fact that Aria was tied up and at his mercy, *he* was the one who felt raw and vulnerable.

Eons later when he thought he could move, he untied her hands clumsily and pulled the covers over both of them, wanting nothing more than to sleep until morning.

Aria curled into his side, one of her legs trapped between his thighs.

She stroked his chest. "I love you, Ethan." The words were clear and unapologetic. "I truly believe you and I have what it takes to make a go of it. You aren't your father. You're a wonderful, honorable man. Please tell me you love me, too."

If she had doused him with a bucket of icy water, the shock and dismay couldn't have been any greater. He rolled away from her, stumbled out of bed and wrapped the sheet around his waist. "Why the hell do women always have to ruin a good thing?"

They hadn't bothered to turn off the bedside lamp. He had plenty of light to see how Aria's face drained of color. How all the joy and peace and contentment fled, leaving her expression devastated and dull.

"Surely you don't mean that. I *love* you, Ethan. I think I've always loved you, but for the longest time I told myself I had to get over you... I had to move on. But then you dropped back into my life, and it was perfect. It was magic. I want to spend the rest of my life with you. I want to make babies with you. I want to grow old with you."

Her words hammered at him like painful blows. *No. It wasn't possible.* His mother had adored his father and her life had ended up a living hell. Ethan didn't know how to give Aria what she wanted. And he couldn't risk it.

"I think you should sleep in your own room," he said. "And perhaps you shouldn't cancel that hotel reservation after all."

Without looking at her again, he strode into the bathroom.

When he came back to the bedroom, she was gone.

The morning following the debacle with Aria, Ethan had a vitally important meeting with two influential investors. It had been orchestrated by Sterling Perry and was not optional.

These two men, whoever they were, had offered to donate huge sums of money to the new club in exchange for having something named after them, like a dining room or ballroom.

Ethan was in a foul mood when he walked into the meeting, and things disintegrated even more when he saw that one of the two men was Harmon Porter. The second fellow was one of Sterling's contemporaries whom Ethan did not know.

Harmon's sneering smile threatened to blow the top off Ethan's head. Ethan hadn't slept more than two hours the night before. He had assumed Aria would go to her room and leave at daybreak. Instead, he had heard her walk out at three in the morning.

By the time he realized what was happening, he had been naked and groggy and unable to follow her.

He felt guilty and angry and even more guilty for feeling angry.

With a manufactured smile for Sterling's friend, Ethan gave a vastly edited version of his presentation and thanked both men for their generosity. He also showed them the list of choices for where their money could go.

Sterling's friend made his goodbyes and left happy.

Harmon Porter lingered. Aria's rejected suitor wore an air of triumph that first puzzled then enraged Ethan.

Porter preened. "Payback's a bitch, Barringer. Here's how this is going to go down. You're going to tell your parents that the only reason Aria agreed to be your fiancée is because she needed your money to get out of her father's obligation. Which makes her an opportunist any way you want to look at it. And make sure they know her poor weasel of a father is an addict who would sell his own daughter to the highest bidder."

"You son of a bitch."

"It's all true." Porter sneered. "That's why there's no ring. I'm not stupid. I've been following the two of you around to see if you were really an item. But you haven't even made a pretense of putting a diamond on her finger."

"And if I don't tell them?"

"Then I pull out of this deal. Sterling Perry will be

embarrassed and kick you to the curb. And your whole house of cards comes tumbling down."

"Go to hell, Porter." Ethan's fists itched with the urge to rearrange the other man's face. But he didn't want to go to jail, and Harmon Porter was just the kind of vindictive bastard to press charges.

Porter walked toward the door. "I'll give you forty-eight hours to think about it. But know this, Barringer. I never bluff. You took what was mine. So it's my turn to ruin *you*."

Ethan didn't care about himself so much, but he couldn't stand the thought that Harmon might humiliate Aria. She had suffered enough because of her father's selfishness.

His gut ached with the realization that Harmon Porter was no better or worse than Ethan. For a man who claimed to care for Aria and want the best for her, Ethan had been cavalier with her heart and her feelings.

Again, he heard her voice inside his head. *I love you, Ethan*. The words had terrified him.

But was there a tiny part of him that wanted to believe he could say them in return? A man who would pledge himself to protect Aria from the Harmon Porters of the world?

After Porter's departure, Ethan wandered the streets of Houston for hours. His phone buzzed and dinged with texts and phone calls. He ignored them all. Inside his chest, a terrible aching void grew and intensified.

He didn't know what to do. The memory of Aria's face haunted him. The worst part was that she had looked exactly as devastated as he remembered his mother being when his father had treated her like garbage.

So what did that make Ethan? He had told himself he was doing the right thing. The safe thing. And yet, he had ended up hurting Aria, anyway.

Harmon Porter's empty threats were nothing to him. Ethan's mother and stepfather would never think ill of Aria. But Ethan did need to tell them the truth before Porter could find some way to cause even more trouble than he already had.

It was starting to get dark when Ethan found himself in front of the hotel where his parents were staying one more night before returning to Royal. They were back from San Francisco and had hoped to have dinner with Ethan and Aria.

Ethan had put them off with a vague excuse.

Now he walked into the lobby and picked up a house phone to ring the room. If they weren't there, he didn't want to deal with another barrage of texts and calls.

His mother answered almost immediately. After a brief conversation, he hung up and headed for the bar, where he snagged a table in a dark corner. He didn't have long to wait. Minutes later his mother, her expression anxious, hurried across the room with John at her heels.

Ethan stood up to greet her with a hug. He shook John's hand. The older man pulled him close and embraced him. The generous gesture threatened to shatter Ethan's fragile composure.

Sarabeth and John sat down opposite him. His

mother leaned forward, her eyes filled with concern. "What's going on, son? Where's Aria?"

He swallowed hard. "I don't know."

And then he told them everything. He told them about Aria's father and the gambling and Harmon Porter. He told them about the money he had paid to Harmon and his pretense at an engagement to appease his mother's concerns that he wasn't settling down.

He stopped short of mentioning the amazing sex and Aria's declaration of love and the way he had kicked her out of his life.

His mother's visible disappointment was a bitter pill. "Oh, Ethan. You've really screwed this one up, haven't you?"

Even John seemed shocked.

Ethan hunched his shoulders. His mother was always on his side. To hear her speak so judgmentally made his stomach tighten. "I was trying to do the right thing."

Sarabeth shook her head. "No," she said. "I think you were trying to hedge your bets. You were scared, and you didn't want anyone to know. You were always that way, even as a little boy."

"I couldn't let Aria marry that weasel Porter."

"Of course you couldn't. And why is that, son?"

He gaped at her. "Because she deserves better."

"That's not why," she said. "You paid the money, because you wanted Aria for yourself."

Ethan felt as if he was on the witness stand. His mother's clear-eyed gaze judged him and found him wanting. "That's not true. I told her from the beginning that it was only temporary."

"And how did this *temporary* engagement work out for you?"

He swallowed hard. "You don't understand."

"Then explain it to me, son."

He searched for the right words. "I remember you telling me that you adored my father from the moment you met. That you fell head over heels. That you thought he was the great love of your life. But it was all a lie. And you suffered. I saw you. For years. I'd rather never have Aria at all than do that to her."

His mother's expression flickered. "Are you telling me Aria loves you?"

"She says she does."

"And what did you say in return?"

He swallowed hard. "I told her to get out of my life."

Even John flinched.

Sarabeth groaned. "Oh, my poor baby. Listen to me. And listen well. You are *not* your father. There are several clinical definitions for what he is, among them a narcissist…a con man. I was very young, and too clueless to see through the act to the real person. Aria, on the other hand, has known you for years. We all know and love you, Ethan. Your family and your friends and your business associates. If you were going to follow in your father's footsteps, it would already have happened long before now."

Ethan stared at her in shock. He had never heard her speak so vehemently nor so plainly. "I see."

"I'm not sure you do. I had no idea you were walking around all this time with the sword of Damocles dangling over your head. Tell me something, Ethan. How many women have you slept with?"

His face flamed. "Uh…"

She rolled her eyes. "A round number will do."

"Ten. Maybe a dozen."

"Okay. And out of that number, how many did you really care for deeply? How many did you worry about hurting? How many did you want to protect and cosset and keep from harm?"

He clenched his jaw so hard his head ached. "One." *Only one…*

His mother's eyes filled with tears, with aching regret. "That's what I thought. That's what I was afraid of. And I suppose that's on me. I didn't realize what my experience had done to you. I tried for so long not to let you know what kind of man your father was, but maybe I did you a disservice. By the time you found out, you were at such a vulnerable age. Oh, Ethan. You've wasted so much time. You love Aria, don't you?"

He opened his mouth to deny it, but the words wouldn't come. His throat was constricted. His stomach felt funny. He felt as if a giant boulder had been lifted off his back. The knowledge that his mother believed for a certainty that he didn't carry the seeds of his father's selfish, callous personality freed him. But at the same time, nothing could undo the consequences of his recent behavior with Aria.

He wet his lips and tried again. "Yes. I love her." He hadn't admitted it until then, not even to himself.

"Then go to her, Ethan. Make this right."

"She may not listen. I hurt her badly."

For the first time, John spoke. "Then grovel if you have to. But make her understand. When you find the woman who is your other half, you have to move heaven and earth to make her yours."

Eighteen

Ethan left the hotel in a daze. He knew Aria planned to return to Royal in the morning. Though it made no sense, he had the strongest feeling he couldn't let her leave Houston without resolving this thing between them. That if she left, and he hadn't made things right, he would never have another chance. It would be over.

Her hotel was four blocks away from the one where his mother and John were staying. He walked there on autopilot. His brain created and discarded one speech after another.

A smart man would go into a big apology with an honest-to-God engagement ring. But all the shops were closed, and he knew he dared not wait any longer to make amends. So there he was. On his own. With nothing but his words and his genuine remorse to pave his way.

The manager of this particular hotel was actually a friend of his. For a split second, it occurred to Ethan that he could probably wheedle a key from his buddy by spinning a tale about wanting to surprise his fiancée. But he had skirted the truth too many times already. Besides, he didn't want to disrespect Aria, particularly not during such a critical moment.

He paced the lobby for five minutes until the concierge gave him a disapproving frown. In the end, he did have to call in a small favor when it occurred to him he had no way of knowing Aria's room number. His manager friend bent the rules enough to give him that information.

Not that it would do Ethan any good. He didn't have much hope that Aria was going to allow him inside.

He rode the elevator to the fourteenth floor, got off and found the correct room. With a quick prayer that he wouldn't say something stupid, he knocked.

The door had a privacy fish-eye.

Moments later, Aria's muffled voice answered. "Go away."

"I need to talk to you," he said. "It's important."

Long silence. "No."

He glanced up and down the hall. "Five minutes. Hear me out. After that, I'll leave. I swear. Please, Aria."

This time the silence was endless. At last, he heard the click as the dead bolt turned and the chain latch was disengaged.

The door swung inward. Aria stepped back to allow him to enter. It was late. She had either showered already, or she had simply been relaxing in front of the

TV. She was wearing soft cotton sleep pants that rode low on her hips and a thin silky tank top that outlined her breasts to perfection.

He had to drag away his gaze, but when he focused on her face, he saw that she had been crying. Her red-rimmed eyes were the worst punishment he could have imagined. His heart fell to his knees.

"I came to apologize," he said.

She shrugged, her arms wrapped around her waist. "Apology accepted."

There was not a flicker of emotion on her face. Not pain. Not joy. Nothing.

"You don't understand," he said, feeling frustration tighten his gut. That, and fear.

"Does it really matter?" Her gaze was bleak. "I don't hold grudges, Ethan. You can go back to your life and everything will be like it was."

"No," he said hoarsely. "It won't."

Aria was close to collapse. Or shattering into a million wretched pieces that she could never put back together. If Ethan needed closure, she would give it to him, but this dreadful confrontation mustn't stretch out much longer. She couldn't bear it.

Though it took every bit of emotional strength she possessed, she summoned a faint smile. "I'm fine, you're fine. Everything is fine. We tried an experiment, and it failed. I don't blame you. Honestly, I don't."

His face was stark. "I love you, Aria."

She recoiled. The pain was intense. "Don't," she said. "Don't say that. You want me. That's not the same thing.

I'm sorry to say I didn't fully understand the difference, but I do now. This is over, Ethan. Please go."

He wrapped his arms around her, burying his face against her neck. "I didn't know," he groaned. "I swear to God I didn't know I loved you. I'd lied to myself for so long about what you meant to me that when the feelings intensified, I told myself it was nothing more than great sex. In my gut I knew that was wrong, but I was clinging to an old lie, determined to protect you from *me*. I couldn't bear the thought that I might be like my father."

She pushed at his shoulder until he released her. Then she crossed to the window, unable to be close to him. Aching from the raw torment of his touch. "How do you know you're not?"

He rose to his feet, his expression agonized. "Because it's been you for a long time now. Years, in fact. No other woman has ever tempted me to contemplate the future."

She had bitten down so hard on her bottom lip that she tasted blood. "We've had incredible sex, Ethan. Off the charts. But married sex is different over a long relationship. If you're counting on the physical stuff to carry us through, it won't be the same. You and I won't be the same. Just go. Please. I release you. Whatever guilt you feel is absolved."

"I can't go," he said. He looked as miserable as she felt. "I love you, and I've hurt you. That was the very thing I *didn't* want to do."

"What makes you think you love me? This is quite a turnaround." His reaction last night when she bravely told him the truth was not something she would soon forget. His angry words had flayed her, opening her to the bone, leaving her emotions raw.

His chest heaved. "When I heard you leave in the middle of the night, I felt like you had taken everything I ever cared about with you. All the happiness, the joy, the contentment. It was all gone. And then this evening, after a particularly unpleasant conversation with my mother, it was brought to my attention that I might be particularly good at deluding myself."

"Oh?"

"She pointed out that I didn't give Harmon Porter that money to help your father or to save you from a bad marriage."

"Then why did you?"

He crossed the room and took her hands in his, leaving her nowhere to go. "I paid the two-point-five million because I wanted you for myself."

Everything she had ever wanted to see blazed in his eyes. Love. Passionate hunger. Unabashed commitment.

"I'm scared," she whispered. "Scared this isn't real."

His expression softened. "You're the bravest woman I've ever met. I'm a clueless idiot, darlin', but if you'll give me another chance, I swear I won't hurt you again."

He pulled her close, stroking her hair and whispering words of comfort. She couldn't stop shaking.

"You don't have to marry me," she said. "I don't want to be something or somebody you're going to regret."

"We're going to have it all, my love. Rings. Vows. Babies. Forever." He found her lips and kissed her long and deep.

It wasn't her imagination this time. Ethan loved her. She felt it in every touch, every whispered caress. The knowledge was almost too wonderful to bear.

The last of her heartbreak winnowed away, evaporating in the bright, hot, perfect bliss of his body pressed against hers. "I love you, Ethan."

He shuddered in her arms, his face buried in her neck. "This time it's forever. You and me. As long as we both shall live."

"Yes," she whispered. "Forever."

He lifted his head at last, his eyes damp. "Thank you for believing. Thank you for not giving up on me."

She kissed him gently, feeling the simmer and sting of passion as it began to grow inevitably. "There was never anybody else," she said. "Not really. From the first moment I stopped thinking of you as just a friend— when I was barely sixteen—I knew I wanted you to be mine."

"Well, you've got me," he said with a wry grin. "I hope you know what you're doing." He scooped her up and carried her the half-dozen steps to the bed. "Do you have an early flight?"

Aria shook her head. "Not anymore, cowboy. I'm all yours."

He glanced over at the half-packed suitcase. "And the black gloves?"

"I thought you'd never ask."

* * * * *

Who is the villain behind it all?
Will Sterling and Ryder ever see eye to eye?

Keep reading
Texas Cattleman's Club: Houston
to find out what happens when a storm rolls in and
reveals secrets meant to stay hidden!

Wild Ride Rancher
by USA TODAY *bestselling author Maureen Child*
is available April 2019!

#2653 NEED ME, COWBOY

Copper Ridge • by Maisey Yates

Unfairly labeled by his family's dark reputation, brooding rancher Levi Tucker is done playing by the rules. He demands a new mansion designed by famous architect Faith Grayson, an innocent beauty he would only corrupt...but he *must* have her.

#2654 WILD RIDE RANCHER

Texas Cattleman's Club: Houston • by Maureen Child

Rancher Liam Morrow doesn't trust rich beauty Chloe Hemsworth *or* want to deal with her new business. But when they're trapped by a flash flood, heated debates turn into a wild affair. For the next two weeks, can she prove him wrong without falling for him?

#2655 TEMPORARY TO TEMPTED

The Bachelor Pact • by Jessica Lemmon

Andrea *really* regrets bribing a hot stranger to be her fake wedding date... especially because he's her new boss! But Gage offers a deal: he'll do it in exchange for her not quitting. As long as love isn't involved, he's game...except he can't resist her!

#2656 HIS FOR ONE NIGHT

First Family of Rodeo • by Sarah M. Anderson

When a surprise reunion leads to a one-night stand with Nashville sweetheart Brooke, Flash wants to turn one night into more... But when the rodeo star learns she's been hiding his child, can he trust her, especially when he's made big mistakes of his own?

#2657 ENGAGING THE ENEMY

The Bourbon Brothers • by Reese Ryan

Sexy Parker Abbott wants *more* of her family's land? Kayleigh Jemison refuses—unless he pays double *and* plays her fake boyfriend to trick her ex. Money is no problem, but can he afford desiring the beautiful woman who hates everything his family represents?

#2658 VENGEFUL VOWS

Marriage at First Sight • by Yvonne Lindsay

Peyton wants revenge on Galen's family. And she'll get it through an arranged marriage between them. But Galen is not what she expected, and soon she's sharing his bed and his life...until secrets come to light that will change everything!

Get 4 FREE REWARDS!

We'll send you 2 FREE Books
plus 2 FREE Mystery Gifts.

Harlequin® Desire books feature heroes who have it all: wealth, status, incredible good looks... everything but the right woman.

FREE
Value Over
$20

SPECIAL EXCERPT FROM

HARLEQUIN

Desire

*Unfairly labeled by his family's dark reputation,
brooding rancher Levi Tucker is done playing by the
rules. He demands a new mansion designed by famous
architect Faith Grayson, an innocent beauty he would
only corrupt…but he* must *have her.*

Read on for a sneak peek at
Need Me, Cowboy
by New York Times *bestselling author Maisey Yates!*

Faith had designed buildings that had changed skylines, and she'd done homes for the rich and the famous.

Levi Tucker was something else. He was infamous.

The self-made millionaire who had spent the past five years in prison and was now digging his way back…

He wanted her. And yeah, it interested her.

She let out a long, slow breath as she rounded the final curve on the mountain driveway, the vacant lot coming into view. But it wasn't the lot, or the scenery surrounding it, that stood out in her vision first and foremost. No, it was the man, with his hands shoved into the pockets of his battered jeans, worn cowboy boots on his feet. He had on a black T-shirt, in spite of the morning chill, and a black cowboy hat was pressed firmly on his head.

She had researched him, obviously. She knew what he looked like, but she supposed she hadn't had a sense of…the scale of him.

Strange, because she was usually pretty good at picking up on those kinds of things in photographs.

And yet, she had not been able to accurately form a picture of the man in her mind. And when she got out of the car, she was struck by the way he seemed to fill this vast, empty space.

That also didn't make any sense.

He was big. Over six feet and with broad shoulders, but he didn't fill this space. Not literally.

But she could feel his presence as soon as the cold air wrapped itself around her body upon exiting the car.

And when his ice-blue eyes connected with hers, she drew in a breath. She was certain he filled her lungs, too.

Because that air no longer felt cold. It felt hot. Impossibly so.

Because those blue eyes burned with something.

Rage. Anger.

Not at her—in fact, his expression seemed almost friendly.

But there was something simmering beneath the surface…and it had touched her already.

Don't miss what happens next!
Need Me, Cowboy
by New York Times *bestselling author Maisey Yates.*

Available April 2019 wherever
Harlequin® Desire books and ebooks are sold.

www.Harlequin.com

Want to give in to temptation with
steamy tales of irresistible desire?

Check out **Harlequin® Presents®**,
Harlequin® Desire and
Harlequin® Kimani™ Romance books!

New books available every month!

CONNECT WITH US AT:

Facebook.com/groups/HarlequinConnection

Facebook.com/HarlequinBooks

Twitter.com/HarlequinBooks

Instagram.com/HarlequinBooks

Pinterest.com/HarlequinBooks

ReaderService.com

**ROMANCE WHEN
YOU NEED IT**

PGENRE2018

Love Harlequin romance?

DISCOVER.

Be the first to find out about promotions, news and exclusive content!

f Facebook.com/HarlequinBooks

y Twitter.com/HarlequinBooks

O Instagram.com/HarlequinBooks

P Pinterest.com/HarlequinBooks

ReaderService.com

EXPLORE.

Sign up for the Harlequin e-newsletter and download a free book from any series at **TryHarlequin.com.**

CONNECT.

Join our Harlequin community to share your thoughts and connect with other romance readers!
Facebook.com/groups/HarlequinConnection

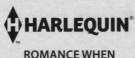

HARLEQUIN®

**ROMANCE WHEN
YOU NEED IT**

HSOCIAL2018

THE WORLD IS BETTER WITH

Romance

Harlequin has everything from contemporary, passionate and heartwarming to suspenseful and inspirational stories.

Whatever your mood, we have a romance just for you!

Connect with us to find your next great read, special offers and more.

⊕ HARLEQUIN®

A *Romance* FOR EVERY MOOD™

www.Harlequin.com

SERIESHALOAD2015

lover in you!

Earn points on your purchase of new Harlequin books from participating retailers.

Turn your points into **FREE BOOKS** of your choice!

Join for FREE today at
www.HarlequinMyRewards.com.

Harlequin My Rewards is a free program (no fees) without any commitments or obligations.